Alexander Snegirev was born in 1980 in Moscow. He studied architecture but then switched to political science. Currently he works in construction design.

He won the Debut Prize for his collected stories *Russian Rhymes* in 2005. His short novel *How We Bombed America* won the Crown Prize of the Writers' Union in 2007. His latest novel, *Vanity,* was named the best book of 2010.

His story "Don't be Afraid, Girl" came out in German in *Junge russische Literatur* (Deutscher Taschenbuch Verlag). "D.R." was included in *Rasskazy*: *New Fiction from a New Russia* (Tin House Books, 2009)

First published in Russian in 2008, *Petroleum Venus* was shortlisted for the National Bestseller Prize, nominated for the Russian Booker, and was on the ozon.ru bestseller list for a year.

GLAS NEW RUSSIAN WRITING

contemporary Russian literature

in English translation

Volume 56

This is the sixth volume in the Glas sub-series devoted to young Russian authors, winners and finalists of the Debut Prize sponsored by the Pokolenie Foundation for humanitarian projects. Glas acknowledges their generous support in publishing this book.

ALEXANDER SNEGIREV

Petroleum Venus

a novel

Translated by Arch Tait

GLAS PUBLISHERS
tel./fax: +7(495)441-9157
perova@glas.msk.su
www.glas.msk.su

DISTRIBUTION

In North America
Consortium Book Sales and Distribution
tel: 800-283-3572; fax: 800-351-5073
orderentry@perseusbooks.com
www.cbsd.com

In the UK
CENTRAL BOOKS
orders@centralbooks.com
www.centralbooks.com
Direct orders: INPRESS
Tel: 0191 229 9555
customerservices@inpressbooks.co.uk
www.inpressbooks.co.uk

Within Russia
Jupiter-Impex
www.jupiterbooks.ru

Editors: Natasha Perova & Joanne Turnbull
Cover design by Igor Satanovsky
Camera-ready copy: Tatiana Shaposhnikova

paper book ISBN 978-5-7172-0096-7
ebook ISBN 978-5-7172-0102-5
© Alexander Snegirev 2012
© Glas New Russian Writing 2012
© English translation: Arch Tait 2012
No part of this book may be used or reproduced in any
manner without the written permission of the publisher.

Petroleum Venus

For my family

Part One

"Turn-key Ham-mam," Vanya reads syllable by syllable as we drive past warehouses festooned with advertisements. To read the signs, he has to flatten his face against the side window and try to catch the letters as they flash by.

"What is ham-mam?"

"A Turkish bath."

"Ham-mam, ham-mam, hammam!"Vanya acclimatizes himself to the new word.

"And what does 'turn-key' mean?"

"They'll completely build the hammam for you and hand you the key. Then all you do is go in and steam yourself. In the hammam."

"In the hammam," Vanya repeats. "Ham-mama!"

The word has taken his fancy. He tests it out, saying it in every possible way, in a high-pitched voice, in a deep, bass voice, stretching the sounds out or saying it very quickly. "Ham-mama, ha-a-a-m-a-a-m-m-m-a-a-ah, hmama!"

Our dour, taciturn truck driver turns up the radio. Vanya rises to the challenge: "Hammam, hammam, hammam!" he yells, leaning over me, to the driver. "Hammam," I respond in a squeaky voice, pulling at the corners of my eyes to make me look like a Chinaman.

"Hammam!" Vanya hoots menacingly in my face, making big, round eyes.

"Hey, not so much noise!" the driver finally barks. He is about to spit, but changes his mind.

I pull another face, as if I am terribly scared. Vanya guffaws. We drive the rest of the way without incident until we can see the old fence of my parents' dacha.

"Stop here," I tell the driver. "The ground isn't frozen. We don't want to get stuck."

"Open the gate," he grunts. We can perfectly well carry things from the truck to the house without driving on to the wet grass. Although it is early December, the weather is as warm as April.

"We really will get stuck. It's happened many times before."

"I know what I'm doing!" In the driver's eyes we are two complete imbeciles. How would we know whether or not he can drive in?

"You muthn't. The wheelth will get thtuck," Vanya intervenes, tugging at his ear and looking down to one side. He always lisps when he's agitated.

The driver growls menacingly. I shrug. "Okay, Vanya, the man knows best. Out we get."

Vanya finds the handle, pulls it towards him, and the door opens. Panting, he tumbles out of the cab. "It's wet!"

"Here's the key, Vanya. Unlock the gate."

Removal drivers are a breed apart. Nobody gets to tell them what they can or can't do. When I was a kid, my parents needed a van to move some old furniture. The driver ignored my father's instructions and we had to get a tractor to pull him out. Five years ago, when we were repairing the foundations, a driver ignored our warning and drove his truck loaded with sand straight in when it was actually raining. He was stuck till evening. We had to dig out all four wheels. You can still see the ruts.

I take the padlock off the gate. The truck drives over the grass to the house. As it reaches the porch, the wheels get stuck. The driver puts his foot down. The wheels spin. "One more smartass," I think as I walk slowly by. The driver jumps down from the cab and walks round, inspecting wheels which have sunk to a third of their depth into the damp soil.

"We'll unload first and then tow it out." I'm in charge now. After all, I'm paying for the delivery and unloading. He finally spits grumpily, pulls back the tarpaulin, and we start unloading bits and pieces of furniture from my grandmother's apartment. There are two old, dark brown beds, a big old dressing table with a serious crack, a stool, a standard lamp, and a polished Romanian chest of drawers. I take the headboard of one of the beds, go up the steps, and cross the verandah. Vanya is rooting about at the front door.

"Dad, the lock is broken!"

"Let me have a go." I put down the headboard, press my shoulder against the door, and turn the key. "You just need to lean on it a bit."

There have been problems with this door before. I brought a girlfriend here one time for a romantic weekend but our plans were nearly thwarted because the verandah had subsided. A broad floorboard had rucked up and we couldn't get the door open. For two days we had to climb in through the window, although actually we were hardly ever out of the bedroom. That doesn't happen any more. My parents had the foundations repaired and the flooring stays where it should. The door is just old and willful.

We go into the cool, dark house, to be greeted by a pungent smell of apples. In September, Vanya and I spread the harvest out over the floor. We take some back each time to the city.

"Open the shutters," I direct. The driver squeezes in, both arms clutching the Romanian chest of drawers.

"Where do I put this?"

"Over there." I nod towards a place by the wall, under a faded Renoir reproduction.

Some naked crumpet is sitting on a bed which is in disarray. She is half turned towards the viewer. All the colours except blue had faded by the time I was born. The blue ink Soviet printers used lasted best. You'd have thought it would have been the ideologically correct red. Details like that caused the collapse of the Soviet Union. The crumpet's face and hair are like my mother's. When I was little, I thought it was a portrait of her. Memories come flooding back, but I quickly hull them, Chernobyl-like, in a concrete sarcophagus and push them over the edge of an imaginary abyss.

Within ten minutes, the driver and I have the entire load in the house. I settle up with him and he goes back to his truck to decide how to get it out of the waterlogged ground. "It's your own fault, pal!" I think to myself. "You were told to stay on the road. All you've done is churn up our grass."

There is no sign of Vanya. One of the blue shutters is half open, the others are still closed. He must have run off while we were unloading. I expect he's out at the road again, collecting whatever he finds. The verge is like a sea shore, where there is always a chance he'll come across something interesting. Broken bits of car lights, wheel trims, and, if he's really lucky, even intact side mirrors. Vanya already has quite a collection. He's insisting his finds all have to go to our apartment in Moscow, while I'm doing my best to make sure they stay here in the shed.

I release catches and tug at unyielding window frames. I unbolt shutters and jolt sash windows. Nature has reduced its palette of many colours to hues of brown and purple. The ground is etched in with dry grass. The magpies' feathers gleam like dark blue silk framing a white shirtfront. By the neighbour's fence, a few dry stalks of lovage are as tall as a person. Each has a large coronet flower-head and stalks like arms raised at its sides. Collectively they look like a crowd of old friends rushing with open arms to embrace each other. The trunks of the pines and aspens exude a velvety dampness. They look as if they have been cut out of textured paper and pasted on to the landscape. In the summer, the trees dry out in the sun, become tinged with ginger, and start showing wrinkles and cracks, like human beings past their first youth. For now, however, confusing winter with spring, they are soft and vulnerable.

Through another window, I see the rickety woodshed with a ladder leaning against it; the ravine overgrown with willows; and beyond it a bend in the road which Vanya particularly favours. The branches merge into the haze. Directly in front of the verandah is the truck, its nose burrowed into the ground.

I put on the kettle and set about lighting the old stove. The house has central heating, but without a stove burning you haven't got a real dacha. Admiring the fire as it begins to take I see a spider scrambling frantically on one of the logs. The poor thing had hidden in a crack and is now trying to escape. I reach forward to pull the log and the spider out of the fire-box, but it suddenly springs into the inferno.

The early winter twilight is falling. The truck's axle bearings grind desperately. My vindictiveness sated, I go out to help.

"Not getting anywhere?"

"It's skidding, damn the brute! Summer tyres. The ground's as soft as snot."

"You need some bricks there."

"Wood is better." The driver starts shoving chocks from the woodshed under his wheels. He starts the engine. I know you need to use bricks. The wheels spin. The wood is just as slippery as the ground.

"I'm telling you, you need bricks."

"The jack just sinks into the ground," the driver complains, but his tone is becoming submissive. Not long now before he does as he is told.

"Put a plank there."

With so many mule-headed drivers around, you inevitably become expert at extricating vehicles from mud. It's not that difficult, as long as you're not in too much of a hurry. If the driver had raised all four wheels in the first place, instead of just the rear ones, and if he'd pushed bricks under them instead of slippery birch logs, he would have been on his way back home by now.

For the first time today, he actually listens to my advice, crawls under the chassis of his truck, which by now has sunk even deeper into the mud, and starts jacking it up. In the meantime I bring up a few bricks which were stacked neatly to one side. Many years ago, they were brought here from the ruins of a church. They are large and still have a three-century layer of old lime, which makes them look like Italian loaves sprinkled with flour.

Vanya skips past holding a frame of some kind, a good half meter by a meter in size. It doesn't look like just another of his treasures washed up by the waves of passing traffic. Perhaps he found it on the rubbish tip in the ravine.

"Have some tea!" I shout after him.

A wheel has been raised above the muddy rut made by its tire. My fingers are frozen and feel as if hundreds of blunt needles are being pushed into them. I take off my jacket to make it easier to work. The wind blows through my sweater. I look at the sky. For days it has been covered with a grey shroud, but suddenly, as the sun is setting, that is dissipating. Above the forest, a pink lake edged with gold appears.

"Hand!" the driver shouts. I barely have time to pull my hand away. The jack has slipped and, as it falls, the wheel snaps a brick in half. There hadn't been time to get it firmly bedded.

From above, I hear a droning which grows louder.

The belly of a plane, tinged by golden rays, appears and disappears in the low ragged clouds like a big fish. I often used to fly and look down at the tiny houses below. Now, I am below, my frozen fingers scraping at the soil beneath the wheels of someone else's truck. Up there, passengers try to swallow hard in order to equalize the pressure in their ears, waiting for flight attendants to serve them a meal, looking forward to holidays, business negotiations, shopping, adultery, and meeting their loved ones.

"Lower away!" The driver released the jack and his truck sank heavily on to the bricks. Some cracked.

The lake of fire iced over as the sky darkened. The sound of a siren came from the direction of the road.

"All sorted!" the driver for some reason shouted with servile jubilation, bringing to mind a spaniel wagging its stump of a tail as it brings back a winged duck.

"Start her up. I'll give you a push!" I pressed against the mud-spattered bumper. "One, two, heave!" I ordered myself. The engine roared, the truck lurched and leaped forward.

"Go! Go!" He drove through the gate and, without braking, headed off.

"Well, so long then!" I waved goodbye to the empty road and was immediately embarrassed at my muddle-headedness. I looked around, hoping no one had noticed me wave goodbye to a driver who had ignored me. There was no one about. I locked the gate and, shaking off the dirt from my hands, went back in to the dacha.

Vanya was busy with something over by the wall. A strip of light strayed out from the partly open bathroom doorway.

"Vanya, why are you sitting in the dark?"

"I'm looking at the picture," he replied imperturbably.

"What picture?" What new fantasy was this? I went over and put a hand on his shoulder.

The picture frame he had brought in from the road was propped up against our pot-bellied fridge. It had a picture in it. I flicked the switch and warm light flooded from our tumbler-like lampshades. A naked blonde, her upturned face registering delight, was squirming erotically while pouring a black liquid, evidently oil, over herself from a red plastic canister. The oil was running over her half-parted lips, sumptuous breasts, and belly button, and dripping from her delta. It streamed down long legs to red stiletto heels. Behind the nude were birch trees and oil rigs, and above the Petroleum Venus's head hovered a halo of golded barbed wire. Her eyes gazed heavenwards, the halo reminiscent of a crown of thorns.

The painting was wrapped in polythene. Vanya had torn a large hole in it without removing it completely. I peeled back the bottom right corner to reveal the name, "Georges Sazonoff", ornately signed in Latin letters.

"It's art!" Vanya said proudly. "Look at the glass I found!" he added, waving a shard of red brake light in the air.

I stood that December evening in the living room of our suburban Moscow dacha, contemplating a painting by a fashionable artist which my fifteen-year-old son with Down syndrome had just dragged in from who knows where.

***

One morning the previous June, my mother had called me to drive her into Moscow straight away for an ultrasound scan. It was an emergency. Where my mother was concerned, everything was. She couldn't do anything without an accompanying hullabaloo. On this occasion, moreover, she was acting on instructions from her pendulum. The pendulum: her wedding ring on a string, provided a definitive answer to any question, and she invariably consulted it. If the ring spun clockwise, that meant "yes"; counter-clockwise meant "no". This time, the pendulum had warned that she urgently needed to have an ultrasound. Urgently! That she had a cancerous tumour, no less.

As my car wound through the villages on the way to my parents' dacha, I was thinking about my impending departure. I'd settle back in a comfortable business class seat, stretch my legs, and fly away. I had an excellent commission to design a villa for rich Russians living in Miami. That humid, subtropical climate, a vast mansion with its own quay, flowering shrubs, luxurious lawns. I had five days till takeoff, a two-year US visa in my passport, and the printout of my ticket in the glove box.

Soon I was driving along overgrown lanes past the old dachas, and then there was the familiar picket fence. Layers of paint blistered and burst from underneath each other. The fence looked like a party of drunks, one board keeling to the right, another to the left, while a third had been ousted by the frost in some long-past winter and pointed straight up.

Vanya ran out joyfully to the gates, like a caged bear cub which sees the zookeeper bringing food.

"Hello! Hello!"

"Hello! Could you open the gate for me?"

Vanya tried to open one side of the double gate but it had sagged and was catching on the ground.

"You need to lift it," he instructed himself and, making a great effort, tugged it upwards. After much grunting, the way was cleared for my Volkswagen.

"Can I drive with you?" Vanya asked, desperately eager to get into the car.

"Welcome!" I said in English.

He became defensive, like a beetle prodded with a twig, uncertain whether the word meant he could get into the car or not. He wasn't to know that mentally I already had one foot in Miami.

"Come on in!"

Vanya got into the passenger seat and started feeling about underneath it for the lever. The seat was too far back. Olga has long legs. I started the car.

"Wait, I haven't got my seatbelt fastened yet!" Vanya protested.

"We're only driving two metres."

"I'll get fined!"

I had to stop to help Vanya find the slot for the seatbelt and move the seat forward until he was comfortable. I was just about to take off the handbrake when he demanded music. We couldn't move until we found a song about a girl who fell in love with a bullfighter. Vanya turned the volume up all the way.

"How are things at work?" he yelled, to make himself heard above the singer.

In order not to wreck my vocal cords, I gave a thumbs-up. I didn't like my family asking me about my work, and Vanya wanted to know about everything, just like my mother. He liked to know and he liked to give advice. That was just like her too. I undid Vanya's seatbelt for him and got out of the car.

"Hi, Mum." A peck on her cool cheek. My mother had grown old. Wrinkles and a stoop.

"Hello." She had a cold and was clearly not in a good mood. She looked tense, displeased about something. Her nose was blocked.

My father came down the verandah steps. A well-built man with a grey crew cut. A colonel friend gave him some khaki trousers from the war in Afghanistan. At the dacha my father was never out of them, which made him look like a gallant retired officer, even though he'd never been in the army. He smiled.

"Hi, Dad." The stubble on his cheek was prickly, as it used to be when he kissed me as a child before I went to bed. Now though, he was subjected, instead of a child's smooth cheek, to my own bristles.

"Are you well?" my mother asked.

"Fine."

"You've got nothing round your throat. You'll catch cold!"

My mother pulled my unbuttoned shirt collar closed. I pushed her hand away. Since childhood, I've hated that feeling of busy fingers at my throat, like insects.

"Are you saying the prayer on page 200?"

She had recently provided me with a curious prayer book which originated from some ancient church, in a modern edition, of course. On page 200 there was a prayer she considered particularly pertinent. "I do not cause others to weep, do not take milk from a child, and obey my parents in all things." Actually, in the book the word "parents" was something else, which my mother had very thoroughly crossed out. I tried for a long time to read it by holding the page up to the light, and finally made out "obey God in all things".

"I am."

"Are you really saying it or just telling me you do?" she queried relentlessly. By "parents", of course, she meant herself.

"Galya, don't start all that again," my father said, touching her elbow.

"You stay out of this!"

My mother gave up her job to care for Vanya, and got into religion, fortune telling, and conversing with Supreme

Cosmic Forces. Answers from the latter were communicated via the pendulum. Until recently, she had been remitting good money to a healer called Semenkov for "remotely healing" Vanya. She had made the acquaintance of Irina, a former accountant who was now a clairvoyant, and would often reverently recount the lady's life history. "Irina's mother was a witch. When Irina refused to become a witch herself, her mother programmed her with black magic spells and nearly killed her. Irina was clinically dead, but recovered. She spoke to Jesus Christ and he told her it was not yet time for her to die, and that she had a mission on Earth."

"What a great swing that is!" I exclaimed with exaggerated enthusiasm, to change the subject. Vanya immediately plonked himself down on it and started swinging to demonstrate its merits.

"My pendulum tells me someone has put a spell on you," my mother informed me over the screeching of the swing's bolts. "I didn't believe in anything either when I was young. Only God can help. Pray to God. You have many sins. I have already freed you from four hundred, no, seven hundred sins from your past lives. I am cleansing your karma, but you have to pray too."

"Mum, I do pray."

"You're just like your father! You don't believe in anything! That's why you aren't well. Your face is covered in pimples!"

"What pimples?" I instinctively felt my cheeks. "Are you crazy? I cut myself shaving!"

She would have liked everyone around her to be ill so that she would have been proved right. We should have listened to her, said our prayers, and worn amulets.

Our relationship had not changed over the years: my mother provoked me to rudeness. I'd say something I shouldn't have, feel guilty, and apologize. How many times I told myself not to react to her sermonizing, just agree with everything she said, and quietly go my own way. It never worked. She always managed to wrong-foot me.

"I have established your sins from past lives: fornication, treachery... and all because you do not believe in God!"

"What makes you think you know whether I do?" I exploded. "God! You're a fine initiate! Perhaps he doesn't exist at all!" Uh-oh. Shouldn't have said that.

Vanya hates quarrels. He's hiding on the verandah with his hands over his ears.

"What do you mean, he doesn't exist? You need to pray! Dear Jesus Christ, help me, please... and so on! Do you pray?"

"Oh, get lost!"

"Fyodor, don't be rude to your mother!" My father's face darkened and his eyes were bobbling alarmingly. I've inherited my lack of backbone from him. Waving my arms I ran into the garden, past the old greenhouse which had been converted into a summerhouse, past the beds of carrots and the garden frame with tomatoes, past the gnarled apple trees with the bark peeling off them like the paint on the fence and the dacha's blue shutters. Beyond the apple trees were the pines and aspens, their trunks as rough and wrinkled as the skin on their owners' faces.

I kicked the first thing I happened upon, a metal toy truck. It flew up and into a pane on the greenhouse. Crash, tinkle-tinkle. I hurt my toe. My anger subsided in a flash. I rubbed my toe, squatted down, and took the truck in my arms like a baby. It was rusty and squeaked morosely. Sorry, old pal.

Soon I would be out of all this. For several whole months I would be thousands of miles away. I went back to the house. My father and Vanya were sitting on the bench, my mother was nowhere to be seen.

"Go easy on her. It's her nerves. You have to be understanding," Father said, with the kind of furrowed brow people affect when speaking of something very minor.

I sat down beside them. Three men, three generations of the family sitting on the old wooden steps of a house built by their ancestor, my grandfather, my father's father, Vanya's great-grandfather. He was a war hero, a general. Awarded this plot of land in the late 1940s, he built the house on it. Most of the ground floor is a spacious living room. Next to it is what used to be my room and was now my mother's room, in which Vanya slept too, and the kitchen and toilet with a shower. On the next floor there are two bedrooms, one was my father's and the other unused, just full of junk. The spacious summer verandah is glassed in with diamond glazing. In the middle of it, a round table is covered with faded oilcloth depicting pears and watermelons. There are sagging wicker chairs around it.

"When is she going to be ready?" I asked my father.

"Any minute. She has to take castor oil before the ultrasound. Want some tea?"

"Why castor oil?"

"It's a laxative. I was sent off to get it from the chemist's as a matter of urgency."

I snorted, to register contempt for the bees in her bonnet. "She'll outlast all of us!" My father stood up, groaning, clutching his back, went to the table to pour me a glass of tea, and offered me some curd cheese fritters.

"I've just made them. Try one."

Delicious, as always. My father was expert at making them.

"Vanya and I are going to get a job as yard sweepers."

He put an arm round Vanya, whose face lit up with the kind of ear-to-ear grin you usually only find on a snowman.

"Yard sweepers? Where?"

"At the Méditerranée."

The Méditerranée is a French restaurant in a side wing of my parents' apartment block in Moscow.

"I like everything to be clean," Vanya said, signaling his commitment.

"Have you bought your tickets?" my father asked.

"I'm flying in five days."

Mum came out to the verandah and asked my father: "You don't know where I put the oil, do you?"

"I gave it to you."

"Because of you I've forgotten where I put it."

"I don't suppose that would be it, would it?" I pointed to a medicine bottle hidden behind a jar of jam.

"Give it here." I passed her the bottle. Without looking at it she began unscrewing the cap.

"You'll be telling me off again, of course, but I've found out why all this happened." We're about to be told again what caused Vanya's illness, I thought with immense indifference.

"There's a curse on his family!" my mother pronounced, pointing at my father. "They had sorcerers among their relatives."

"Here we go again," my father said with a long sigh and patted me on the knee.

"And also Lena had an Andrei of some description who was in love with her and cast a spell."

"What Andrei? Why would he want to cast a spell?"

"Fyodor, can you at least not rise to the bait?"

"I don't know what Andrei! My pendulum told me. He did it out of jealousy."

"That was all fifteen years ago! Fifteen! What right do you have to keep talking about God when you don't have a trace of humility? You don't listen to anyone but yourself! What does that make you?"

My mother looked at me like a saint defamed and downed the bottle of medicine in one.

For a moment there was nothing strange. She screwed up her face, but that didn't seem odd, castor oil is not to everyone's taste. But then she became ashen-faced and stared at us crazily with wide open eyes. A strange smell spread.

"What's wrong? Do you want me to pat you on the back?"

Instead of answering, my mother gulped painfully for air. It wasn't like breathing even, more an odd noise in her throat.

"Mum, what's the matter?" We jumped up.

"I can't see properly."

"What can't you see?"

The bottle fell from her hand and rolled across the verandah, counting the floorboards. She started to collapse. I barely had time to catch her and fell to my knees under the weight of her body.

"What's wrong with you? What are you feeling?" I was sure this was just more of her silliness, to show us all how much suffering we caused her.

"I... can't see... call the ambulance..." A strong smell of medicine and hospitals was coming from her. That smell!

"Holy shit! We need an ambulance," I repeated, pressing the keys on my telephone with trembling fingers. "Where's the number of the rapid response service? What have you taken?"

I picked up the bottle and read the label. "Why does it say 'camphor oil' when you took castor oil!"

"You gave me it... water…" Mum whimpered. I grabbed the kettle in which we kept drinking water and brought the spout to her mouth. My father was shouting, my mother sobbing, her teeth rattling on the spout. Vanya was chewing his nails in the corner. If only she'd stop crying, just stop crying. I wanted to kill her or myself, just so as not to hear her crying and gasping.

While I was attempting to get through to the ambulance, we tried to get Mother to drink the water. They told us over the phone it would be at least an hour before any doctor would reach us and we decided to take her to the hospital ourselves. We dragged her to the car, Dad kicking the watering can out of the way. Mum suddenly doubled up and life drained out of her eyes, like water disappearing into sand.

Catastrophic dehydration, they said after the autopsy.

***

My name is Fyodor Ovchinnikov. I am thirty-one and have a degree in Architecture. I was seventeen then, and Lena was a year older. We met in our first year, in the college canteen. We kissed by a fountain. First love. We decided against an abortion. Why Vanya was born with Down syndrome nobody could really explain. It is unusual with young parents. The bald, bespectacled doctor said, "You drew the short straw."

My mother prepared very actively for the birth. She bossed everyone around, even Lena's family, and was dead set against an ultrasound scan on the grounds that it would frighten the baby. We did as we were told. We did have one scan though, at a clinic she recommended. The doctor said, "You are going to have a boy." We decided to call him Vanya.

The baby arrived a month prematurely, but it was a straightforward birth with no complications.

We were at the dacha. Lena woke me up in the night. I ran round to a neighbour who had a phone and called an ambulance. Lena was crying out every half hour, then every fifteen minutes, then every five. We finally realized the baby was being born. There was still no sign of a doctor. Vanya delivered himself without medical assistance. I was the nearest we came to a doctor.

When I saw that slippery little baby, I was trembling with joy. I have a son! I have a son! Then the ambulance arrived. After inspecting the baby, the doctor took me aside and said quietly that there were some question marks. So far, only doubts, nothing more than that. There would need to be tests. The baby's ears were set rather low. The neck was rather squat, and his eyes were slanted.

We were taken to an isolation hospital for people who failed to have their baby, like decent, law-abiding citizens, in a maternity hospital. It was a place mainly for the homeless. I'd heard about it, and begged them to take Vanya and Lena to the regular maternity hospital. I handed over all the money I had on me. The doctor nodded, pocketed the money, and still took us to where we were supposed to go. The nurse immediately removed all Lena's clothes and put her in a faded, ragged smock with no buttons. They took Vanya away to have injections, and for a few minutes more I could hear his fitful crying.

"What are you getting so upset about? He's a mongol anyway," the ward nurse comforted me. A blood test confirmed the doctor's doubts, and a repeat produced the same result.

Many times I dialed the doctor who had carried out the ultrasound examination, only to put down the receiver. I would dial again and put it down again. I finally made up my mind, got through, and asked her why she was so bad at her job. How could she not have noticed such a serious defect? We could have had an abortion instead of giving birth to a defective baby.

"I believe in God," she responded firmly. "I saw you had a Down baby, but you can't kill an innocent child."

At this point, Lena's family seized the initiative. "To have all the pain of looking after an invalid from the age of seventeen? To never have healthy children after that? It will be best all round if the baby dies. Disabled people are a burden on society and a burden to themselves. To help a child like that to die is an act of mercy. Euthanasia of the disabled is illegal, so the best way to hasten its death is to put it in a home."

On her mother's advice, Lena was not breast-feeding Vanya, in order not to bond with him. My parents vacillated. I was totally confused: torn by love for my son, but hating him because he'd spoiled my life at the very outset.

Lena agreed at once. I thought about it for a short time, smashed a chair on the floor, threw the telephone at the wall, and decided to abandon my son. In the town hall we signed a formal document renouncing parental rights. We told friends the baby had been stillborn.

The first few days, Lena and I went to see Vanya at the hospital. They didn't want to let me even into the waiting room. It was against the rules. We bought the guard a bottle of vodka and that was the last we saw of him. The nurse said the ward was draughty and Vanya would need warm socks. We bought socks. By the next day, someone had stolen them. We bought him some more. A week later, my mum got over the shock and took Vanya away from the hospital. My dad had doubts, but didn't argue.

I was tormented by a smell. Lena smelled the same as the son we had abandoned. The smell of our crime gave me no peace. She felt disgraced because she had been unable to produce a "normal" first baby. She couldn't bear to see me because she felt she had brought me ill-luck. She left. I was alone in my grandmother's apartment.

***

Tearing off the rest of the polythene to take a closer look at Vanya's find, I saw it was a genuine oil painting. While its artistic merit might be debatable, it was by an artist whose work was in demand and commanded a good price. Some of my clients had commissioned Sazonoff to paint them dressed as one of Napoleon's marshals; or to paint their children, wives, or lovers as Greek deities; and sometimes to paint group portraits of their entire business team in the style of Rembrandt's "Night Watch".

Our curvacious blonde would not have been out of place painted on the door of a long-distance truck, with her voluptuous breasts, diminutive waist, the canister in her hands the same red colour as her nails and stilettos, and the oil spattered over her body like the sperm of some primeval monster from the bowels of the earth.

Vanya could not take his eyes off the painting. He stared at the woman's white body dripping with black oil.

"Vanya, can you please tell me where you found this, er, painting?"

"I won't! I won't!" he shouted, running round the room laughing, and flung himself down on the high-backed sofa with its threadbare velvet bolsters.

"Come on, Vanya. Tell me."

He suddenly started bawling. It's something he does. "M-m-mmmmm, don't ye-ell at me-e-eeeee! Wa-a-aaaaa!" He was instantly transformed into a big baby in floods of tears and smearing snot all over his face.

"I'm not yelling at you! Stop howling. You're grown up now!" I tried to maintain my pose of a firm but fair father.

"Ah-ah-ah-aaaaaaaa!" His mouth and nose bubbled.

"Well, all right, I'm sorry... I'm sorry, pal, I just... like... I'm sorry!" I'm a useless nanny. I gave Vanya a hug and patted him on the back. "Don't cry. I'm asking for a reason. It's a bit weird. I'm just pushing that truck out through the gates and you suddenly bring back a painting. What if there are gangsters looking for it?"

"It's pretty," Vanya snuffled. Like a baby, he stops crying as quickly as he starts. I wish I was as easily placated. If I get stirred up about something, I take ages to calm down again. "Go on, tell me where you found it."

"I won't!"

"Did you find it at the rubbish tip?"

"I won't say! I won't say."

"Come on, then, you can show me," I said gently, and took him firmly by the hand. I put on his jacket and shoes. He didn't resist. I put on my own things and we went out to the road.

***

From the outset, Vanya was different in every way from normal children, even in his physical proportions. Ordinary children are like pretty dolls, with a head, arms, and legs all the right size. Vanya, though, looked like a teddy bear, his arms and legs too thin, and his head and belly too big. The doctors predicted an early death. His heart had serious defects, he was physically weak, and tended to catch colds. He didn't learn to walk until he was three and a half. But he lived.

I couldn't get my head round the fact that I had a mentally retarded son. I was a young guy and just could not accept it. I lied to friends who lived in the apartments on our staircase, people I'd known since I was little. I told them that, because our baby died, my parents had adopted someone else's baby with a disability. I was terribly ashamed of Vanya. I couldn't imagine admitting I was the father of a Down syndrome child. My own parents had me late in life. As a child, I overheard a conversation between my mother and a doctor and found out that she'd had something called resuscitation of the foetus, i.e., me. They had revived me with an injection. I was stillborn, almost. As a child, I was often ill. I had rickets, a large head, a bloated abdomen. I was constantly being dragged off to see doctors.

Because of curvature of the spine, I was forbidden to lift weights, and my mother couldn't think of a better way to help than tearing up my schoolbooks so I only had to carry in my briefcase the pages I needed at a particular time. "You ought to be ashamed of yourself! This is a book!" Every day I was reprimanded by my infallible Soviet schoolteacher and endured the derisive laughter of the boys and, worse, girls in my class. My grandmother would take me to school and collect me after school, long after other children my age were coming and going on their own. To cap it all, I had a lisp. After much shrieking, tantrums and threats, I managed to get my grandmother's escort duty cancelled, but in retaliation had a bunch of house keys hung round my neck on the grounds that otherwise I might lose them. Those jangling keys were a millstone dragging me down to a watery grave.

As a teenager, I secretly took up sport. Secretly, because my mother forbade me to strain myself on account of my weak heart. In the mornings, I would leave home early, and learned to do pull-ups on the horizontal bar in the courtyard. Once my father found me out, but he didn't blab to my mother. Instead, he made a pull-ups chart for me on squared paper. After two months, I could do ten pull-ups, stopped handing in medical certificates exempting me from physical education, and sailed through all the school's medical tests. The PE teacher even sent me to compete in the district cross-country run, and I came second. My dad fixed it for me to see a speech therapist.

In the course of a single summer, I became physically strong, learned to pronounce "r" properly, and gained a whole lot in self-confidence. I discovered I had a sense of humour, and that girls fancied me. I became the life and soul of the party, graduated from high school and went to college. I developed a great aversion to disabled people, cripples, or weaklings. Life was just taking off when, – wham! I had a half-witted son.

***

Why I am getting so wound up over this painting? Okay, so it's by Sazonoff! So what! Why should I care where Vanya got it from? Why are we in such a hurry to go out to an empty road this December evening? It is ridiculous even to think of trying to find the painting's owner. I'm so intense about everything. I end up obsessively doing pointless things, but I suppose living with Vanya would drive anyone round the bend. On auto-pilot, however, we go out. The few streetlights are turned on, and twenty metres down the road, our neighbour Victor Timofeyich is standing by his gate.

"Good evening, Victor Timofeyich."

"Hello, Vanya. There's been an accident, did you hear?"

"Yes," Vanya squeaks.

I squeeze his hand hard, suspecting a connection between the accident and the painting.

"What kind of accident?"

"A Toyota came off the road at the bend. The ambulance

has just taken the driver away. He was drunk. I talked to the cops. Who sells these people their driving licenses? I'd shoot them myself!" Victor lights a cigarette. "Tell me, Fyodor, what kind of people are these? There's always been a road sign there to warn there's a dangerous bend coming up, but they hurtle into it like maniacs and fly head over heels. Drunk or sobre seems to make no difference!"

"Perhaps they don't believe the sign," Vanya suggests.

"Perhaps they don't." Victor Timofeyich sighs heavily. "One moment you are whizzing along and then bang, that's the end of you. Go and take a look. I imagine his car is still there. The car's mug was all smashed in!"

"We'll go and take a look."

"Goodbye, Victor Timofeyich."

"Take care, Vanya."

When we are out of earshot, I ask Vanya about the accident. He looks shifty, and starts rubbing his left hand with his right, as if washing it.

We climb down into the ravine. Pushing the willow branches away from my face, I notice the catkins are beginning to swell. Stumbling over bags of rubbish, we climb up the other side to the road. Blue lights are flashing on police cars. A police Lada is at the roadside and a Toyota, its front crumpled like paper, is emphatically stationary in front of a leaning pole. Fragments of the car's lights are scattered over the roadway like confetti, and the ground is stained black with leaked oil.

"Did the painting come from the car?" I ask quietly.

"Yes…"

Should I tell a cop before it's too late? What if something else is missing, money? In fact you can bet your life there will be. The doctors may have helped themselves, or the cops, and they'll blame it on Vanya.

We stand on the verge, like two natives who've come out to gawp at a tanker which has foundered on the reefs. Already we're attracting the attention of a cop in the car. Don't want to make him suspicious. I try to make it look as if we are just out for a walk. Perhaps we make a habit of coming out to the road of an evening to watch the traffic.

We retreat back into the ravine. Vanya murmurs something under his breath. Great! It would appear my mentally defective son has just robbed a dying man.

***

For the first few months after Vanya's arrival, I didn't know what to do with myself. I even prayed in church one time for him to die. "Take Vanya, O Lord." Vanya lived.

"What have I done to deserve this? Why am I being punished? I've only recently become normal myself!" In order for God not to think me self-centered, I made the request on behalf of my parents. "How are they to blame? My mother has worked from morning till night all her life. She so wanted a grandson. My dad is a decent, honest man. So why this? Well, okay, Lord, but what about Vanya? When he grows up, he is going to know he is not like other people, that he can't think as clearly as they do, and that people are laughing at him."

I advanced many arguments, but to no avail. Then I got shirty with God. "You know, God, either you don't exist or you are a really stupid cunt! And don't think you can blackmail me! Keep your magic aura for the idiots who believe in you. That woman doctor, for instance. I'll do as I see fit! My life belongs to me, get it?"

My mother gave up her job and devoted herself to trying to heal Vanya. She believed Down syndrome was curable. "I asked the angel, and he said when Vanya grows up he'll be a general, but for that to happen we have to pray tirelessly." My mum had unbelievable faith in her dogmas. She even consecrated the apartment, using some ritual she had invented.

I used to argue with her. When Dad was there, he would insist I mustn't be rude. Little Vanya was frightened by loud voices and wailed. That was always how things developed, on the rare occasions when we met.

As the years passed, Vanya's Down syndrome showed no sign of being healed. I got quite well established as an interior designer of private homes. I even found the situation had its plus side. If I'd had a healthy baby, I'd have to look after him and not had enough time for a career and for diversions. As a regular client, Mum got a gift from Semenkov, her faith healer. It was a gadget for shaving those little pellets off woollen clothing.

She spent all her spare time looking for reasons why Vanya was born that way. When she was young, she'd been a Communist Party functionary, so deciding who was to blame was second nature. One time, she would reproach me for having let Lena catch cold in the first month of pregnancy. The next, she would find a hex on my astral body. I couldn't stand her preaching, but neither could I get by without her. We were like lovers, always having it out with each other. At the beginning of every visit, we would get along fine. In the middle, we would almost be ready to fly at each other with our fists. At the end, we would either be kissing each other a fond farewell, or my mother would be standing looking tragic, her arms dangling listlessly, as I stormed out slamming the door.

My father just accepted life as it was. Vanya was the apple of his eye. He would rock him in his arms, play with him with wooden blocks, read books to him, and make up funny songs. I kept meaning to record him on tape but never got round to it, and then there was no one to record.

After Mum died, the police arrived to investigate whether the poisoning was homicide. The idea even crossed my mind that my father might have put the oil there on purpose. My mother used to nag him relentlessly. It would have been the perfect murder, looking as if the sales assistant in the chemist's shop had made a mistake. The victim drank it herself. No one forced her to. I was a witness to that. I never got to quiz Dad about it. He died of a heart attack the day after he was questioned by the investigator. How the camphor oil got switched for castor oil, nobody bothered to ask. They put it down to a tragic accident and closed the case.

***

We sit at the round table and look at the painting in silence.

"I was walking along and then, bang! The car had an accident! I went over. The man wasn't moving. He hadn't done up his seat belt. You should always wear your seat belt…"

"Tell me about the picture."

"It was next to him. I opened the door and took it."

"And nobody saw you?"

"I'm not sure," Vanya says, wondering. How could he have brought the painting all the way home without anyone noticing? All we need is for a witness to turn up. The painting is crap and not worth a lot of risk.

"Dad, is it art?"

"Art? Oh, well, it's difficult to say. Probably not exactly."

"Why?"

"Well, for a painting to be considered art, it has to

be... it has to be..." I hesitate, not finding it easy to explain something so obvious. "Art has to be beautiful. There!"

"But is it ugly?" Vanya asks in surprise. "She is very beautiful!"

I look at the Petroleum Venus. You can't in fairness say she is ugly, but something like that just doesn't get called beautiful. "Perhaps it is beautiful. Oh, I don't know."

"What is art for?" Vanya persists.

"What do you mean? Well, so you can show other people something you think is beautiful. That sort of thing. Say an artist sees a beautiful woman, he paints her, and it turns out you think she is beautiful too."

Vanya opens his eyes wide and covers his mouth with his hands, the way cartoons convey astonishment.

"I get it."

"What do you get?"

"The painter painted it specially for me!"

"No, Vanya. That's not what I meant..." But he is not listening.

"I get it! I get it! He painted her for me!"

I stop listening to Vanya and try to imagine who this Venus could belong to. Some oink got rich and commissioned a painting of his mistress? A widowed forty-something decided to ask a fashionable artist to paint her portrait? Or had "Sazonoff" taken it into his head to create a new image of Russia, as a curvacious blonde, with oil and birch trees?

***

After my parents died, I returned to the ancestral home. Everything seemed strange. Here is where I kissed Lena for the first time. Here is the piano beneath which we embraced. The on-off light on the TV was still covered over with insulation tape, because my mother had established with the aid of her pendulum that the TV used that bulb to suck energy out of people. The parquet flooring had pencil markings indicating energy fault lines. I walked around the room disconsolately, while from behind the big glass door my halfwit son, wearing one of my old T-shirts, watched me warily.

I was a hostage of my parents' virtue. A disabled dependant is like stocks on your feet, a prison for those around him. You can't go out, can't travel. All you can do is sit with him and empty his chamber pot. My parents decide they will bring up Vanya, and then, wham, they die almost simultaneously. So what has any of that to do with me? Okay, so he was my son, but I repudiated him fifteen years ago. He has no father! There is even a stroke through the space for "Father" on his birth certificate. Why is he sticking to me like a wet leaf? My life has been derailed. My thoughts turned to my mother.

"You bitch! You utter bitch! You wanted a grandson? Well, you got one. Wasn't that enough? Even now you're dead, you want to force me to carry on living by your rules. No way!" I hissed, kicking the armchair. "I wasn't born dead just to be buried alive thirty years later!" Or perhaps I never was born. Perhaps those obstetricians at the maternity hospital didn't succeed in resuscitating me and I'm dead and have been incarnated in some alternative, warped, wrong world.

Having deposited my parents' bodies at the crematorium, I decided I would quickly put my son in a special home and hope still to make it to Miami. I put Vanya in the car and we went off to get it over with.

Driving along a narrow street, we saw a large creature in an old nylon anorak with a hat pulled down over its eyes in spite of the heat. The creature was sluggishly shambling along the pavement, and boys were jumping around firing plastic pellets at it from toy guns.

"Go away! Scram! Fire!" their ringleader shouted spiritedly.

When we were closer, I could see the creature's face. It was a feeble-minded tramp and the kids were hunting him as if he were an ancient mammoth. He responded to their gunfire and yelling with inarticulate grunts and, clumsily shielding himself with his arm, continued on his way. I thought I should probably chase the boys away, but heard the car door slam, a screech of brakes, and furious honking. Vanya had jumped out of the car and nearly been run over by a bus.

"I urge you to disperse!" he shouted to the boys, breathing heavily. The boys stopped in their tracks and took a look at this unexpected intercessor.

"Keep out of this, roly-poly, or we'll drill you too!" their leader threatened, recovering his wits. The whole gang joined in, jeering.

I turned on the hazard lights, leapt out on to the pavement, elbowed Vanya aside, and went for the boys. They took to their heels. I picked up a beer bottle lying next to a rubbish bin and chucked it after them. The glass exploded on the roadway next to one of the fugitives. Vanya pulled another bottle out of the bin, threw it wide, and hit the feeble-minded man he was supposed to be defending. The tramp grunted and crawled off through the bushes, out of harm's way. Vanya was about to rush apologetically after him, but I caught him by the edge of his shirt. The boys stopped some distance off, looking back anxiously.

We got back in the car. My knees and hands were shaking, my heart pounding, my teeth chattering. I managed somehow to start the engine and did a U-turn. My destiny was suddenly staring me right in the face, like during rush hour in the metro when people you have never seen before and who are standing some way off are suddenly pressed up against you. Like it or not, you can't help noticing the pimples, the pores, the hairs on the cheek of the woman next to you, who shortly before had seemed flawlessly beautiful. Now it was my destiny which was right in front of my nose, breathing in my face. I could smell it. I had been trying not to look at it for a long time, but now had no choice but to see it. Contrary to my fears, the sudden proximity did not make it seem hideous. You can be afraid of something, and then, when push comes to shove, it turns out not to be all that intimidating. I suddenly recognized it was time to stop running away from my destiny and what it offered.

***

We spent a week at the dacha as planned. The doctor had said Vanya needed fresh air. The time passed uneventfully: nobody came looking for the painting.

We were standing at the bus stop. It was still warm. The wheels of passing cars were sending spray in our direction. Every now and then, I hauled Vanya back from the edge of the road, when he moved forward to look out for the bus. Finally, our 112 approached. We paid the driver and squeezed inside.

I've started copying some of Vanya's quirks. For example, pulling faces, deliberately frowning, and sticking my tongue out as if I'm being over-diligent. I walk like a duck, looking around earnestly. Why? I expect I'm subconsciously showing solidarity. It's a bit like when you are going upstairs behind some crippled, injured person on crutches and can't get by. Your first reaction is irritation at being abruptly slowed down, but then you remember your standards of public morality and reproach yourself for being so insensitive. When you finally reach the top of the stairs and could speed up and take off, you're suddenly in no hurry. You carry on hobbling along next to the cripple. Why? It's somehow embarrassing to show off what your legs can do to someone who doesn't have any, or not any that are fully functional. It would be a bit like flashing your money in front of a beggar. Of course, the feeling wears off after a few steps. The disabled person is left behind and you go forward, speeding up, your embarrassment and sympathy are dissipated.

At that moment, though, when you stop being in a rush to get past, unhurriedness suddenly suffuses you. You feel the attraction of jerky motion, and realize that this too is a way of living; a different way, viewed from a different perspective. You find it interesting to live this way, subordinate in status to somebody disabled, become his friend, disciple, apostle. Born healthy, you voluntarily choose the lot of a cripple.

I wanted to "get past" Vanya, to run away from him as fast as I could. But I couldn't do that, and now I'm pretending to be ill. Look, everybody! I'm behaving like someone who's mentally retarded! Everyone thinks it's terrible to have Down syndrome, so let them look at me! I'm a cool guy and I'm pulling faces by choice.

The bus passengers divide into those who pretend not to notice us and those who stare at us wide-eyed. People feel they ought to pretend disabled people are not there, but secretly they want to look at them, like animals in the zoo or their own shit. I've got used to it. Invariably, if I look round, several people look away. Some who have no manners stare openly and whisper. For the first month, I saw every such stare as a challenge. I stared back at these insolent types so fiercely that they looked down cravenly.

Since then, I've become more tolerant. Let them look if they want to. Who cares? Older women silently commiserate; men timorously make way; girls examine the pair of us with a mixture of curiosity and hostility: an unshaven guy in a hoody and a Down syndrome teenager with ash-blond hair and a backpack.

Because he's been eagerly pushing his way to the window, Vanya is drooling. I point this out to him, so he takes out a handkerchief and wipes his face. Settling by the window, we look at the houses along the roadside flashing by, the woodland, and filling stations.

"Su-per-mar-ket, wheel ba-lan-cing, pa-lat-i-al fur-ni-ture." The latter signboard, made of large plastic letters, adorns the facade of a run-down two-storey prefabricated building. Next to it is a red sign, which Vanya reads out for the whole bus to hear:

"Ero-tic shop! What does 'ero-tic' mean?"

"It... well... they sell... various things for living."

"Why haven't we been there? Let's go there!" The passengers standing nearby want to laugh but, bless them, keep a straight face. It's not done to laugh at the afflicted. "We'll go there some time," I say with a grin.

"Why are you laughing?" Vanya asks defensively. One thing he doesn't like is people laughing at him.

"I am laughing because I love you," I say, putting an arm round him.

I bet many of the bus passengers are wondering how they would behave if fate tied them to someone with Down. Would they look after them or put them in a home? The sight of us makes people think about big issues. They feel sorry for us. I doubt whether anyone guesses how often I reproach my parents for their charitable impulses, which have forced me too to be charitable. They don't know I conceal Vanya from my friends, or how I envy them the, no doubt fleeting but nevertheless alluring, gloss of their well ordered lives. Neither do our fellow passengers know that the tube I am carrying is the rolled up canvas of the Petroleum Venus, removed from its frame and stretcher.

I unlock the apartment door and the thought does cross my mind that the painting's owners may be waiting inside for us. They may have sussed us, broken into the apartment, and be ready to ambush us. I hesitate for a moment, before flinging the door open.

In the window, beyond the four-leaved glass doors of our living room, the lights of the city twinkle. The tower of the Ministry of Foreign Affairs, the statues on the residential building on the far side of the river, the neon sign advertising chicken stock cubes. The window looks like a painting: the drunk artist in the car crash, the "palatial furniture", the erotic shop, and the road sign warning of a dangerous bend which nobody pays any attention to, it's all here, in the world depicted in this real-life painting. Perhaps the God who created the view through that window, the God who created Vanya, perhaps he too is blind drunk. Perhaps, like me, he too just likes pulling silly faces.

***

The apartment is a total mess, with clothes, CDs, and books scattered everywhere. We aspire to wash the dishes at least twice a week, but don't always manage.

Vanya has already unrolled the painting on the floor.

"I'll hide it for now."

Perhaps I'm just telling myself the Venus isn't valuable because I don't want to face the possibility that we have landed ourselves in real danger.

Vanya carries the picture off to his hiding place, an Indian patchwork rug I once brought back for my parents. I bought it off gypsies in Mumbai. Applying the power of prayer, my mother believed she neutralized various negative programs and charms the rug contained, and then hung it in Vanya's room. Patches of bright colour stimulate child development, and the rug consisted entirely of brightly coloured scraps of old saris: muddy pink, bluey green, golden, saffron. The patterns create a world of imaginary plants, suns and stars, ears of corn, crowns, and paisley shapes. There is a pattern like the outline of a body chalked on the ground at a crime scene, only the deceased appears to have had rabbits' ears. I like the squares which form a St Andrew's cross from corner to corner. It's like the flag of the Russian Navy except that, instead of a blue cross on a white field, the cross is made of sequined light green fabric and the background is red and embroidered with suns with curly rays.

Some of the seams between the rug's patches conceal zippers which fasten hidden pockets. Mum sewed them in specially for Vanya. One time, when he was being examined by a doctor, I gave in to temptation and guiltily checked out his treasures. In one pocket he had a collection of pretty candy wrappers and bottle labels, in another a spent rifle cartridge and toy figures from chocolate surprise eggs; in a third, a collection of wheels from toy cars. For some reason he had no interest in the cars themselves. There was a separate Polaroid photo of my parents with Vanya, on the back of which he had printed, "GOD MAIK MUM AND DAD BE IN HEVN THANK YOU IN ADVANCE".

Because of its treasures, the rug weighs the best part of ten kilograms. Vanya asks me not to look, but I know he will try to squeeze the painting into the largest pocket.

"I can't do it!" I soon hear him complain.

"Want me to help?" I ask, tactfully not turning round.

"Yes, please!" Vanya says, forgetting about keeping it secret.

He has already unceremoniously folded the painting in half and then in half again. He has carefully ironed the folds with a heavy English-Russian dictionary. Now when you open the picture out, you see four folds, like on a bedsheet which has lain for a long time in the cupboard. I help him cram the stolen masterpiece into its exotic hiding place.

"Do your best and earn a rest!" Vanya says, rubbing his hands with satisfaction.

***

Each case of Down syndrome presents differently. Vanya's is not one of the most severe. He is not hopelessly dim, and even looks quite cute. If he didn't have that one extra chromosome, he would have hordes of admirers. He is a chubby, green-eyed blond with, for some unknown reason, a rather arrogant expression. The blond hair he gets from my mother: Lena had a mane of auburn hair and mine is brown. Vanya looks around him regally, a Siegfried with Down syndrome, but that expression readily changes to the mischievous grin of a boy who has just surreptitiously wolfed the birthday cake. A prominent feature is his tongue, which he has never learned to keep inside his mouth.

Vanya can't be left alone, and needs to be put to bed. He can't be sent out shopping. He can't even boil an egg. If we are going to be out for more than an hour, I put a nappy on him, just in case. He also looks amazingly like his mother, Lena. There is something of her in his eyes, his cheekbones and lips. He is a replica of her made by a drunken sculptor. The end result of my wonderful love affair. We haven't spoken since, even on the phone. I did dial her number once, but after it had rung a couple of times, I put down the receiver.

Vanya's brain is crammed with two kinds of knowledge. The first is my mother's theories about God, witches, prayers, clairvoyants, and karma. This hotchpotch of beliefs peacefully coexists with information derived from my father's trips with him to museums, and his reading aloud to Vanya of poems and novels. When making sense of the world around him, Vanya selects alternately from these databases and confidently applies whatever he finds to any given situation. In addition, from time to time, he receives advice from an angel.

He is afraid of terrorists, Chechens, and female suicide bombers. The public hysteria about dark-haired enemies in black burkas has produced a unique amalgam. Evil forces like witches have fused in my son's brain with suicide bombers into a single deadly danger.

Vanya only began to recognize me when he was eight. Before that, he was as afraid of me as of anybody else he didn't know. My mother and father had an unspoken convention of not telling Vanya I was his father. Luckily, it has been easy to persuade him otherwise.

"How can I have two dads?" he asked in puzzlement.

"You can, Vanya. Stranger things can happen. One dad is now with God, and the other is right here," I assured him, poking myself in the chest.

"But what will that dad say?" Vanya persisted, pointing upwards.

"My angel says he is okay with it."

When I mentioned the angel, Vanya looked at me with respect and asked no more questions.

Olga, for whose long legs I'd moved back the passenger seat, took one look at Vanya and vamoosed. She gave me to understand this was not how she was intending to live her life. Vanya would be hard work and I was no longer eligible.

She took cancellation of the Miami trip very hard, having planned to go with me for the shopping, the beaches, and luxurious spas.

Those who look after sick people often become very haughty, as if to say, "Look at us. We are sacrificing our lives, abandoning all worldly pleasures for the sake of the afflicted." As far as I am concerned, a carer who gives herself airs because she washes out pus-soaked bandages is no better than some overdressed airhead flaunting her bling. Certainly, I'm no saint. I'm doing this because I can't get out of it. High-minded suffering is not my bag. I don't aim to stand out, or rate myself more highly than other people. It probably is a touching sight, a young man devoting himself to caring for a disabled boy, but I don't need other people's respect and sympathy. I decided not to let new people I meet see my son. It was then I realized that looking after someone disabled is not just a prison, but a prison which carers construct for themselves, walls they build between themselves and the rest of humanity.

When they heard of the choice I'd made, some friends thought I was nuts. Others hinted I was all but a saint. Both groups stopped phoning. I don't blame them. You can't take Vanya to a club, and not everyone would choose to share a table with him in a restaurant. He is quite likely to laugh too loudly, or to display the half-chewed contents of his mouth when he wants to say something. Fair enough. Why test them to destruction?

***

Vanya and I are walking along a wet path in the cemetery. Unswept leaves have been mashed underfoot. The colours are those of dried fruit: melon, papaya, apricots. Where there are too many leaves, our shoes slip. The sky is overcast, the temperature still about ten degrees above zero. Something is happening to Russia's climate. It has been incredibly warm for a month, with no sign of cold weather on the way. The sun has not been showing itself, which upsets Vanya. He isn't happy without the sun.

"Vanya, keep an eye on the numbers or we'll get lost." I haven't been here since I was little, but Vanya came several times with my parents.

"I am keeping an eye on the numbers. We need number 49B!" He waves his hands in the air. There is a mitten on one but not on the other.

"Where's your mitten, Vanya?" Vanya looks at his hand, as if seeing it for the first time, and concludes, "I've lost it."

I sigh. Although it's warm, I'm afraid he might catch cold and I give him my glove.

I'm carrying a heavy parcel containing two urns, my mum's and my dad's, and we have come to the cemetery to bury them. Why only now, six months after they died? My mother long ago gave detailed instructions about how she and my father were to be buried. For Dad the ritual wasn't important, so Mum took charge. The procedure for her burial changed depending on which religious beliefs were currently in favour. At one point, she wanted to be buried in her wedding dress, at another to have a church funeral service and to be in a closed coffin. I was dismissive of her wishes, saying she shouldn't be thinking about death, but couldn't help remembering it all when the time came. Her last instructions had been for her body, clad in a nightgown she had been given by clairvoyant Irina, to be cremated and the ashes buried six months later. She had arrived at that period of time with the assistance of the pendulum. The pendulum, that is, her wedding ring, was to be buried with her. Dad's body was subject to the same rigmarole, only minus the nightgown and pendulum. Meticulous observance of the ritual would ensure some kind of bonus in the next life.

I fulfilled all her requests, except that I forgot the pendulum, and when I did remember it, was reluctant to bury a ring. It was a memento, and, moreover, a memento made of gold. I am hoping this infringement of the prescribed ritual will not doom my mother to eternal torment. For the past six months, we've had the urns on our balcony.

"Forty-nine! Look, there!" Vanya shouts.

"We need 49B."

"Oh, sorry, sorry, I'm being careless. Sorry!"

"No problem, Vanya. It doesn't matter a damn," I reassure him.

"Dad, that's a bad word. Bad words spoil your karma," he says, just like my mother. "Hey, don't tell me what to do, okay?" His face crumples. He's going to cry. "Vanya, I'm sorry. I won't swear. Just don't be upset! Ah, here's the sign!"

At a post marked "49B", we turn right. The path goes downhill. Here is the well, the litter bin, the wrought-iron railing round the moss-covered monument to a heroic pilot. We squeeze past it to our family grave. Vanya's jacket snags on a prong on the pilot's fence and a piece of white polyester padding gets pulled out. I see he is about to start bawling again.

"The jacket doesn't matter a... in the slightest. We'll sew it up, don't get worked up about it." I pat him on the back.

Now taking great care, we continue. We arrive. I look around. Have we come to the wrong place? It seems to be right. There's the huge, decaying tree stump, the heroic pilot. But where is the grave? It's disappeared!

What I mean is that the grave is, of course, still there, but the gravestone to my grandfather and grandmother is missing, and in its place is a fresh mound of earth covered in fir branches and with a temporary marble plaque on a black metal stand.

"Dad... who's that?" Vanya asks.

"Are you sure this is our spot?"

Vanya looks around. "Yes, but where are Grandma and Grandpa?"

"Grandma and Grandpa... Damned if I know!"

"Dad, who is this?"

"I wonder..."

The plaque, inscribed with gold lettering, reads, "Sazonov, Georgy Viktorovich. 1953-2008." Beneath are engraved a paintbrush and an artist's palette.

***

A few days previously, I had typed "Georgy Sazonov" into a search engine and found out a little more. In addition to the fact that Sazonov was a well-known artist who had managed to persuade many affluent neophytes that his works were "must-have", I learned that "Mr Sazonov died a week ago in intensive care after a traffic accident". There was nothing about the disappearance of a painting.

"Have the suicide bombers kidnapped Grandma and Grandpa?" Vanya asks after a pause.

"What suicide bombers?! This is all like some practical fucking joke!"

"Dad, don't swear. God doesn't like it. It creates bad energy which adversely affects your health and..." Vanya hiccups on the word "health", which comes out as "hell-th".

"God again! What is it about this family!" I pull up the plaque with the paintbrush and palette only to see the slab with the photos of my grandparents lying on its side behind the mound of earth.

"Is it a long time since you were last here?"

"I don't remember."

I kick the mound.

"Don't do that! Grandma and Grandpa are in there," Vanya jabbers.

"I just hope they are still there! It looks like your favourite artist has moved in on top of them! What kind of nonsense…" I am ready to weep with impotent rage and despair.

I hear a shout behind my back, "Here's Dadda! Look, here he is!"

We turn round. Two unknown girls are edging in our direction. One is a sleek young madam with brown hair and come-hither eyes, looking a little disheveled. Behind her on tiptoe, trying to step in the less muddy places, skips a leggy blonde in a light coat and high heels.

The girl with brown hair stops and eyes us appraisingly. "Put that plaque back where it belongs, will you?" I remember I am holding the marble plaque bearing the artist's name. "And you, move yourself. Don't stand on our grave," she says, now addressing Vanya. He retreats in alarm.

My irritation erupts with volcanic force. I've needed someone to yell at for a long time and the occasion has now presented itself. Flinging the plaque to the ground, I stamp on it and advance on madam.

"This is our grave. My gran and grandpa are buried here!" I'm immediately embarrassed by that childish "gran and grandpa", but it's too late to take it back.

"I'll thank you not to raise your voice to me!"

"Why did you remove the plaque?" the blonde chips in.

"You've usurped our grave! That is a criminal act... I...

We…" As always when I'm nervous, I start losing my chain of thought and stumble over my words. I've been meaning to go on a public-speaking course but haven't got round to it.

"I have no intention of bandying words with you in this place," Madam cuts me short. "We have bought this plot entirely properly, and what was buried here before is of no interest to us."

"What!... Bought!... What was buried here?!" I splutter.

Vanya is about to start crying again.

"My dear young man, you shouldn't get yourself so worked up or you'll be fathering another halfwit," Madam triumphantly hammers home her final nail.

The blonde behind her looks at the ground.

"Another... halfwit…" I croak. I am so furious, I completely lose my voice. I cannot utter a word. I start coughing. While I am trying to quell the treachery of my voice, my right hand remembers its boxing lessons. I throw a clumsy punch, like in a dream. My fist slithers over her lips, but it is enough. She totters and sits down in the middle of a wreath of plastic roses with a ribbon reading "To Our Much Loved Dadda".

The blonde rushes at me yelling, with the hint of an accent, "How do you dare!"

"Oh, you bastard. I have a meeting in an hour's time!" Madam hisses, wiping a crimson droplet from her rapidly swelling lip. Clutching at the decaying tree stump, she tries to get up but the rotten wood, like a spongy soufflé, gives way and she sits down again. Her skirt rides up, flashing a glimpse of pink panties. The blonde has to come to her aid before she finally gets back up on her high heels, which keep skidding from under her in the mess of wet leaves.

"Sonya, you're okay?" the blonde clucks.

"That faggot has split my lip!"

"Calm yourself," the blonde coos, dusting her down. "Calm yourself. We are all being very impulsive."

Madam comes over to me. "All right, you goat. I'd put you inside if I didn't feel sorry for your pathetic freak!"

I see at unnervingly close range her set of even teeth, their white perfection set off by her split lip. Implants. Knocking one out could set you back 500 euros.

"What did you say…"

I wince as her knee connects forcefully with my balls. Meanwhile, her arms flailing, she again collapses in a heap.

"We'll sort this out through the cemetery office!"

The girls retreat, picking their way past the railings. Madam's ass has leaves and bits of rotten wood still clinging to it. The blonde thinks of something and comes back. She walks carefully round us and places two white roses on the grave.

Vanya and I sit down on the bench by the pilot's fence.

"I got a bit carried away just then."

I take out a handkerchief and wipe Vanya's face. Sniveling, he says, "I don't want to be a halfwit! I don't want to be a freak! I don't want people looking at me! I want to be clever, and handsome, and tall…"

"You aren't a freak, Vanya. It's that bitch is the freak."

"She... she's pretty," Vanya sobs.

"What?"

"She's pretty. And the other one, too."

I see Vanya in a new light. In all the time we've spent together, I've never heard him mention womanly beauty, but now, like a burst of machine gun fire, there has come, first, his enthusiasm for a certain painted lady, and now for the two women who are entirely real.

***

When we had calmed down a bit, Vanya and I decided we should get on and bury the urns. We scooped out two holes in the freshly dug soil with a shovel, and then filled them in. It was as if we were burying thermos flasks rather than two human beings. There was no solemnity about the occasion. While we were doing it, I was thinking that quite clearly the cuckoo in our grave was the painter Vanya had robbed. The year of birth of the Sazonoff in the newspaper coincided with the year on the marble plaque. "Our" Sazonov, like the "well-known artist" Sazonov, had obviously been buried in the last few days. And there was that engraved paintbrush.

Having dispatched the urns, we repaired to the cemetery office to sort out the whole sorry mess. I don't like talking to officials. I don't like officials. I even thought about just leaving everything the way it was, but recognized how irresponsible that would be. A grave is the history of your family. Besides, it costs money. If something happened to me, where would I be buried? Actually, I wouldn't care, but what if Vanya…?

We encountered a surly guard, a queue, and an unscheduled tea break, the traditional trinity of Russian state institutions. We patiently overcame all these obstacles, but didn't get to see the boss. Instead, we were shown in to one of his deputies.

This extremely fat, florid man kicked off by questioning the validity of our rights to the grave and demanded we produce the relevant documents. Trying this time not to get over-excited, I informed our florid friend that not only did we have all the necessary documentation, but also extensive contacts with influential people. Having worked for over a decade in architecture, I could mention several individuals of substance. They were hardly likely to intervene, but entirely serviceable for bluffing purposes.

The florid deputy summoned his boss. The cemetery director looked even more fat, florid, and glum to boot. For these people, happiness is directly proportional to the amount of vodka and kebab they ingest. The director employed a different tactic, reproaching Vanya and me for our negligence and failure to take proper care of the grave. The implication was that, if we had been regular visitors to the cemetery, this would never have happened. The wronged party has to be put in the wrong. It is the girl's fault she gets raped, the driver's that his car gets stolen. After a good talking-to, you slink away as if you have been to confession. Go ye and sin no more.

Doing my best to keep my cool, I reminded both our florid friends that the heirs to a grave do not forfeit their property rights because they haven't been seen visiting it for several years. This was tantamount to violation of the rights of a disabled, under-age boy. It might well be a criminal offence. We parted, agreeing that I would bring my documentation and that the complaint would be investigated.

***

After my Miami commission fell through, others also began to fall away. I could not take Vanya on site visits without scaring off the clients, and I also couldn't entrust him to a nurse. At the beginning, I did try, but within a few days he had become sluggish and dozy. I came back early one time to find the nurse in my bed with a geezer. Vanya was sleeping like a log, the lady having given him tranquillizers, while she entertained her fancy man.

I question my decision every day, especially when I see photos of new buildings and interiors. This was designed by one colleague, that by another. I know them all. Until recently I was working with them, but now... Sometimes, for old times' sake, one will pass something on which I can do at home, but I'm sliding down the scale. An architect needs to be present, and I am chained to Vanya. Before long, I'll be designing interiors for garden sheds.

I even miss having someone to moralize and give me unasked-for advice. Before, I at least got phone calls from my mother, but now there is nothing. In order not to go completely crazy in this enclosed, haunted, space, I take Vanya to museums and exhibitions. He gets concessions. From time to time there are incidents. At the preview of an exhibition of chocolate products at an old confectionery factory, I had only to turn my back for Vanya to tuck in to one of the exhibits. In full view of a goggle-eyed supervisor, he bit off half the corpulent right flank of a chocolate pig. By the time I got over, Vanya, smeared in chocolate, was munching his way towards the tail. While his feeble teeth were ripping its body to pieces, the pig had a wicked smile on its lips and was winking a blue candied eye. We beat a hasty retreat. Since then we visit only non-edible exhibitions.

We live ever more modestly. Shortly after the death of my parents, I was involved in a car crash. I got away with a few bruises, but had to sell the car for scrap. We soon got through my parents' savings. Over the years, they had managed to squirrel away fifteen hundred dollars out of their pension. From force of habit, they had exchanged rubles for dollars and put them in envelopes. Despite earning a decent salary, I hadn't saved a ruble. I blew the lot on restaurants, travel, and clothes. Vanya gets a disability pension. I try not to think about the future.

***

The director of an amateur theatre for young people with mental anomalies phoned. My mother had fixed Vanya up with them. For the past two years he played Mercutio in

"Romeo and Juliet". The director informed me that Vanya's role would be given to another boy.

"Why?"

"Vanya hasn't been coming to rehearsals regularly, and he gets the words wrong."

"He hasn't been missing rehearsals. I take him there myself. He's only missed one, when he had to have an electrocardiogram."

"It's not just that…" The director began talking fairly incoherently about a businesswoman whose son, Kirill, had always dreamed of playing Mercutio, and this lady had promised to give the theatre a suite of furniture to use in their sets.

"We bring our armchair to every performance! My mother sewed costumes for you, and now suddenly some energetic mumsy comes along with her offer of furniture…" I interrupted.

"You have been asked on more than one occasion to leave the chair at the theatre!"

"That armchair is one of Vanya's favourite possessions! I can't just give it away!"

"Well, Kirill's mother evidently can."

I was unable to save Mercutio. Vanya would be allowed to read the epilogue and, by way of compensation for emotional distress, I managed to negotiate him a role as a page. Shakespeare doesn't actually have a page. I made him up as we went along. The page will welcome spectators before the show and announce the interval. I told Vanya it was good for an actor to perform a variety of roles. It could only improve his skill. He was still upset.

"A plague on both your houses!" he exclaimed, assuming a dramatic pose.

I had never been to this production. A company of

adolescents with Down syndrome performing the world's most famous love story is not everybody's cup of tea. I was certainly going to go now, especially as the next show was just coming up.

"The whole problem is me," Vanya announced in an unexpectedly tragic voice.

"I'm sure you play Mercutio very well."

"But I stole that painting and this is God's punishment." Vanya assumes dramatic poses appropriate to the meaning of his words. Now he was sitting there, clutching his head in his hands.

"You said yourself at the dacha that the artist had painted that picture just for you." Vanya did not respond to this observation, and instead said gravely, "We need to go and see Auntie Irina."

"The soothsayer, you mean?" I asked with heavy irony.

"She's been to see Jesus Christ," Vanya said sternly, and I recognized a familiar, sententious tone of voice.

Actually, we didn't have that many options. We had nothing to do, no entertainment, so why not go and see a fortune teller? Especially as I'd never seen the lady before. I found her phone number in my mother's notebook and dialed it.

"Hello," a woman responded huskily.

"I am Fyodor, Galina Ovchinnikova's son."

***

A few months after Vanya was born, I started feeling really, darkly envious of people with healthy children. I would look at pregnant women and hope they too would have handicapped babies. A Down, or a cretin, or at least one which was mentally retarded. It's not that I actually wished harm on anyone; I just didn't want to be alone in my plight.

As if to spite me, everything went fine for all of them. Their brats were thoroughbreds. They grew up and florished. All my friends seemed to do was show me photographs and boast that their children were already beginning to walk, had featured in commercials, were studying at an English special school, and were scraping out scales on the violin.

I couldn't sleep. A dog was howling outside the window, a group of drunks went by, inebriates shouting. Lonely high heels clattered by and were quiet after passing through a gateway.

Try as we may to escape the influence of our parents, we get nowhere. Here I am now, lying in my parents' bed, fulfilling the obligations they took on in respect of Vanya, and about to go to see their clairvoyant.

The rectangular shadows of the window frames and a fantastical cobweb of tree branches run over the ceiling in the white beams of car headlamps. A car drives into the courtyard with electronic music pounding away inside it. What kind of an idiot is that? Everyone is trying to sleep! I bet it's a Lada with tinted windows, blue neon lights, and a raised rear end, racing style. The music becomes appreciably louder as they open the door. I hide my head under the blanket. It doesn't help. I leap out of bed, rush to the window, tug at the frame. I was right, it's a Lada! There it is down at the entrance with its headlights on. I'll tell them! "Hey, you! Keep it down, will you?" The cry is ready to burst out of me. Should I add "you goat"? "Oy, you goat, shut it!" My fingers tug at the window catch...

A girl emerges from the entrance, takes her place in the Lada, slams the door, the music moves away into the distance. "Goats! Bastards!" I yell as loud as I can into the void of the courtyard. They hadn't even the decency to wait for me to swear at them.

The refuse truck arrives. Metal containers are emptied into its orange body with a shattering of bottles. The first trolleybus comes by, its earth lead jingling over the asphalt. Morning has arrived.

But what about God? Now that full responsibility for my son has devolved upon me, now I've had to abandon my career and private life, I have ceased to rail at God. I've just given up on him. For me, God has become something like a figure in those stories about secret societies, books of magic and occult knowledge. All these myths exist only because people are too scared to face the truth, the fact that after death there is NOTHING. I fall asleep.

***

I wake up with a spring-like feeling. The sparrows are chirping in the street and there is that special turmoil normally peculiar to March. I pad barefoot over to the window. The weather continues to amaze. The snow-clearing vehicles are idling under the bridge with nothing to do. The nursery teachers have brought the children out to get some fresh air, and they are twittering in the playground. Toddlers in colourful dungarees are jumping up steps and sliding down chutes, getting themselves stuck between the bars of the fence, and walloping each other with toy spades. One in leopard-coloured overalls has raised a rubbish bin as big as himself and is trying to put it on his head. The teachers, two young girls, sit smoking on a bench, letting the children get on with it.

I hear splashing in the bathroom. On Wednesdays, and today is Wednesday, Vanya has a bath.

"Hi!" I peep in the half-open door.

"Good morning!" Vanya replies happily, sitting in the turquoise water.

Someone told my mother that small doses of copper sulphate kill germs not only on plants but also on human beings. She really hated germs. One New Year's, not wanting to waste the alcohol left in the wine and liqueur glasses, she poured it over the potted plants. Wine and vodka contain carbohydrates, so they are nutritious and, she reasoned, must therefore be good for plants. The main thing, though, was that alcohol kills germs.

The plants were dead before Orthodox Christmas on 7 January. My mother did not accept responsibility, blaming the poor energy emitted by the guests and mistakes she'd made in the proportions because Dad distracted her by talking to her. She performed dubious experiments on a regular basis, mostly on Dad and me, and later on Vanya. We, however, did not die as a result but emerged all the stronger. Copper sulphate was probably the least alarming of her innovations. She treated a sore throat with paraffin oil, and migraine by making healing passes with her hands.

When I was little, my mother put me in the bath and sprinkled in a handful of copper sulphate crystals. The granules sank to the bottom, leaving a bright blue trail. It looked as if magic incense was burning in the water, producing turquoise smoke. I loved that swimming pool colour of southern climes, and for a long time believed that bright blue baths were standard for every Soviet child.

As time passed, my mother's repertoire of techniques for fighting the battle for health evolved, but certain truths remained unchallengeable, including copper sulphate in the bath. Quite apart from killing germs, this useful compound also compensated for any deficiency of copper in the body. When I grew up, mother moved on to Vanya. Her stocks of copper sulphate were extensive.

My mother needed followers. My father always broke

her diets and ridiculed her clairvoyant. I didn't toe the line either. Her ideal disciple was, accordingly, Vanya. She found just what she wanted. Vanya had complete faith in her. He said the prayers she told him to, and did special physical exercises to strengthen his link to the cosmos. Now, his little white body is sticking out of the blue water as he plays with a much chewed plastic duck. The water is a bright spot in his world, second only to the Indian rug.

"When are we getting the new copper sulphate?" Vanya asks unexpectedly. I lift the once heavy bag, examine it, and realize a copper sulphate crisis is imminent. Our stocks, which had seemed inexhaustible, are, of course, as finite as their mistress. "When? Soon. I know where to get it." In reality, I have no idea. Mother used to obtain it by playing on her status as a member of the chemistry institute staff. "You'll have your copper sulphate. We'll get it."

Beneath low cloud, the city looks grey and cheerless.

"Dad, when will the sun come back?"

"You can ask the clairvoyant when we see her."

***

We have a whole class of deaf and dumb students in the railway carriage with us. They communicate energetically with each other using sign language. Some twenty young people chatter away excitedly without uttering a sound, only the slight rustling of their fingers being audible. It is a strange sensation to have people in front of you joking, telling tales about first kisses, and showing off new mobile phones, all without uttering a single word.

"Why are they doing that?" Vanya asks.

"That's how they talk to each other," I reply in an irritated whisper. I feel Vanya is talking too loudly and staring too openly at them.

"Can't they talk like normal people?" Vanya asks more loudly, thinking I can't hear him properly. A woman with a mop of dyed curls casts a stern glance in our direction.

"Not so loud, Vanya! It's not polite to talk about other people in front of them."

"They can't talk! Ha-ha-ha!" Vanya bursts out laughing. Some of the deaf and dumb young people turn out to be dumb but not deaf. They look round. Other, "normal", passengers begin giving us disapproving looks. I'm ready to sink through the floor.

"We're getting out," I say, pushing Vanya out at the next station. "You ought to be ashamed of yourself, laughing at disabled people! It's stupid and disgusting!"

"I'm allowed to. I am stupid. I have Down syndrome!"

"That's a fine excuse! We have to respect other people! Everybody has their faults! You are not only a disgrace to yourself, you disgrace me too!"

"I won't do it again. I'm sorry." Vanya is upset. Any moment now, he will start bawling.

"You've got Down syndrome – how about that! You ought to be grateful I'm always fussing over you, but you want to show you're the tough guy. Just learn to behave like a normal human being!"

"I am normal! I am normal!" Vanya shrieks, tears and snot flying everywhere.

I find a handkerchief and start wiping his face, roughly, hurting him. I almost punch him with the hand holding the handkerchief. Why does he have to bawl his head off all the time! I very soon start feeling sorry for him and ashamed of myself. Absolutely everybody going by turns to look back at us. Fuck them! I don't care if they set out chairs in a row and spectate.

"Forgive me, Vanya. Do you hear? Forgive me. You're

fine. I shouldn't have said that. It was stupid of me," I try to backtrack. "You are my sweet boy. I love you." Vanya gradually calms down and we continue our journey.

***

The green cap of a soft drink bottle is lying on the granite floor of the train terminus. Vanya kicks it and it skids over to me. I feint, a real Brazilian Zidane in front of the goal, and kick it back to him. He misses it, and runs grunting and laughing delightedly after it. It rolls towards a policeman with a moustache who looks at us severely before making a faultless pass to Vanya.

There are a lot of people on the stairs. Their backs are covered in cheap cloth, they have heavy bags in their hands, crying children. Country people, visitors from the South. Our vast country is on the move.

We go out deep into the courtyards of grey, substandard apartment blocks. The washed out, muddy weather typical of Moscow between the seasons. A rat darts out of a rubbish bin down into a basement.

"Look, a rat!" Happily I point my finger, following the rodent's progress.

"Where, where?"

"There, look! It's run away."

"I didn't see it," Vanya laments, as if the appearance of the rat was the second coming of Christ.

"No sweat. You'll see another one."

"Where do rats live?"

"In basements."

"The walls are wafer-thin, the rats gnaw through them and settle in."

The walls of these Khrushchev-era five-storey blocks really are like old, grubby waffles. The concrete panels are faced with tiling. The joins between the panels are outlined in dark filler, like mouldy wafer filling. Tiny balconies sag under the weight of junk: old tires, skis, defunct refrigerators. Wash bowls and sledges are strapped to the outside of the balcony railings. On one, a zebra skin hangs from a clothesline. Perhaps zebras breed around here, not just rats.

Some balconies boast their owners' attempts to glaze them in: crooked, cracked frames that don't fit together, only half the height they need to be, often without glass in them. String bags of groceries hang down from kitchen windows. Crows do their best to pilfer the produce, and then fat, ungainly women, or men in rancid vests, throw open the windows and scare the birds away.

By the entrances, a number of cars are dormant. One or two of them are still on the go, but the wheels of the rest are now bedded in the mud and covered with shroud-like, decaying tarpaulins.

"Dad, is it true Moscow is the most beautiful city in the world?"

I survey the world around me. "Well," I begin, disconcerted. "Maybe not the most beautiful, but certainly one of the most beautiful."

We walk on in silence. Vanya has never seen other cities, but I have. I understand that all this dirt and poverty are not really compatible with beauty, but there is something about the place, something as ambiguous and paradoxically beautiful as the Petroleum Venus. Except that it's not really beauty, but love. Love not of the city, or the country. Just love, love in general.

I walk along next to Vanya, and that feeling grows inside me. Love for those old, abandoned cars whose owners died long ago, for those mouldering joins between the wafer-thin panels, and for the string bags hanging down from the windows. For the first time, love of the world floods over me. Unreserved. Just love.

***

We find the apartment block we are looking for, and then the right entrance. I ask Vanya to press the three greasy buttons of the combination lock simultaneously. When he succeeds and the latch clicks open, I pull the brown metal door open. There is a smell of stagnant water in the stairwell, or perhaps of dead rats decomposing in the basement.

I run up the stairs two at a time, Vanya imitating me. We reach the third floor. The door we need is insulated with black leatherette quilting in a diamond pattern. The clairvoyant has a musical door chime.

"Fyodor?" a woman's voice calls through the door.

"Fyodor and Vanya!" I announce.

Locks click, and in the doorway stands a plump brunette in a garish housecoat.

"How was your journey?"

"Fine."

"We're suffering a fracture in the energy cortex. There's a strong field influencing our legs. Tea, coffee?"

I decline: "Thanks, we had a drink before we left."

"Then come this way," Irina says, inviting us into the living room.

It's hot, and there's a smell of yesterday's soup. The windows are taped to keep out draughts. Irina evidently doesn't believe in ventilation. There is a dark wood wall-unit with a television and a dozen dog-eared romance novels on the shelf, a vase with a peacock feather in it, a hand-coloured photo of a married couple with frozen expressions, and a sofa.

A man is lying on the sofa. He is covered with a net

curtain. A shiver runs down my spine. Without turning round, Irina offers her practised explanation:

"That's my husband. He fell asleep two years ago. Displacement of his energy double plus some karmic sins… certain obligations he had from a past life."

"Oh…," I drawl, looking at Vanya. He might have warned me. He's been here before. Vanya is wearing a serious expression, as if attending a church service.

"So, what were you wanting to ask me?" Irina enquires, getting down to business.

"We happen to have something that belongs to another person, it was an accident. We'd like to give it back and don't know how to go about it. We are beginning to have some difficulties, and we think it's because of that," I explain a little hesitantly.

"Have you brought it with you?"

"Er, yes, as you asked. Vanya, take it out."

Vanya takes the folded painting out of a plastic bag, proudly unfolds it, and shakes it out as one might a tablecloth before putting it on the table. Irina's expression is inscrutable.

"I shall now commence the seance. Please obey me unquestioningly and do not interrupt."

"Of course, yes…" I nod several times.

Irina sits us down on chairs, lights candles, and places the painting before her. She picks up a prism attached to a string, closes her eyes, and enquires, "Pendulum, will you hear me? If yes, swing clockwise."

My eyes are glued to the pendulum. Vanya looks at it, then at me, then back again. This is not his first time. He is feeling knowledgeable. The pendulum circles, at first slowly, then faster. Irina's hand does not move, there is no draught. It is swinging counter-clockwise.

"What is it? Are you unwilling? Are you tired?" Irina asks the pendulum understandingly. "Well, never mind. Take a rest." She holds the prism in her hand and blows on it.

"We'll have to use a different approach. I shall disrobe. Do not be concerned. I shall need your hands."

Before she has finished speaking, her housecoat is on the floor. Vanya gives a vague grunt. Evidently this is not something the clairvoyant has got up to before. I try to retain my composure, although I don't find it easy when confronted with a hefty, completely naked matron of late Balzacian years.

"Hands," Irina commands.

"Mine? Sure... Is mine enough? Vanya, er, well… for him it's a bit... unfamiliar."

"I need a hand of the person who committed the theft," Irina cuts me short. I do not know how good she is as a clairvoyant, but she certainly has a shrewd understanding of people. She sussed us immediately. Vanya doesn't move.

"Give me yours too. He's afraid to do it on his own."

Ashamed of my cold hand, which in addition is sweaty, I do as I am commanded and Vanya follows my example. Irina presses our hands hard against her breasts. We are leaning over awkwardly from our chairs, our faces disagreeably close to the densely overgrown place between her fat legs. It strikes me that, if her husband has now been asleep for a couple of years, this is a neat, official way for her to have contact with men. We can feel her meaty nipples under our fingers. I look out of the corner of my eye at Vanya, who is breathing very rapidly. I just hope he won't have a heart attack, given his congenital defect. Although, on the other hand, it is good if he at least gets to grope a woman before he dies.

At first, Irina moans quite melodiously. I even find

myself drifting off to sleep, but then she suddenly begins speaking, barely intelligibly. "A road... haste... a man is hurrying... a gift... he is bringing a gift... he is late... a bend in the road..." She starts sobbing, and from her closed eyes pour tears black with mascara. "Death! I see death!" As she utters this, Irina opens eyes bulging with horror. "What are you dragging me into?" she yells, pushing us away. "I do not work with deaths!"

Vanya has stopped breathing completely. I am shaking all over. I don't know what is more scary: her sudden yell and the black tears, or the accuracy with which she has described how we came by the painting.

"We haven't killed anyone. It was an accident," I stammer. "Vanya just took the picture without thinking because he liked it. We want to give it back."

"He doesn't!" Irina says, nodding in Vanya's direction as she slips her housecoat back on.

"He likes the painting, but he is willing to return it. Help us. We've been having such difficulties ever since," I plead. "My mother told me so many good things about you!"

"Very well, your hands..." Once again she goes into a trance. "A road... a gift... I see the past... you all have a common past... and future... black, sticky... spray in the face... sun..." Irina squeezes my hand.

"Ah-ah-ah-aaaaaaah!" This time it is Vanya.

"Fuck! It's his heart..." flashes through my mind. I turn, and my hair stands on end.

Instead of Vanya writhing in mid-heart attack, I see the man covered in net curtain slowly rising from the sofa. Her husband! Without using his hands, he just sits up. He continues wearing the net curtain.

"Oh! God!" I shriek, jumping up and pulling my hand away. Seeing her husband, Irina freezes. Without removing the curtain from his head, he enquires, "Irina, do we have visitors?"

Vanya and I rush out to the hallway, pushing and shoving each other as we both try to squeeze through the door. All that has happened is that a husband in a coma has seen fit to wake up in the middle of a session to identify the owners of the Petroleum Venus. Nevertheless, we can't wait to get out of there. You never can tell how a man may react when he wakes up after two years to find a couple of young guys fondling his wife's tits.

We have forgotten the painting! After a moment's hesitation, I rush back into the room, grab the painting, and for some reason say to Irina, "Sorry!" She is sitting motionless, facing her husband.

Grabbing our jackets from the coat stand, trying to shove our feet into our shoes as we run, we push at the door. We can't get it to open... bolts, latches... we push, it doesn't open... I glance round to see the husband's head veiled in net curtain looking in our direction.

I shout, "The money's by the mirror!"

He makes no response. I shouldn't have mentioned the money. He may think his wife has turned to prostitution. Then I nearly collapse under Vanya's weight. He's finally worked out how to open the door, by pulling inwards. Obviously. You don't push, you pull. Only Vanya pulled too hard. It flew open and he fell back on top of me. Grabbing coats from the stand, ripping the tabs for hanging them up, I nearly collapse holding a bunch of old raincoats. I throw them aside and propel Vanya towards our escape route.

***

The estate agent has phoned. I've been trying for the past two months to rent out Grandma's apartment. I desperately need money, but am having no luck: one would-be tenant thought the plumbing was too old-fashioned, others looked dodgy and offered too little. After breaking up with Lena, I didn't carry on living there for long. As soon as I had some earnings, I rented a place of my own. I didn't want to be dependent on my parents. They rented the apartment out from time to time, but didn't refurbish.

"A young woman wants to rent it. She's educated and solvent. Sells paintings. She's looking for a one-room apartment to use for storage."

"Paintings have been bringing me a lot of luck recently," I think wryly.

The next day, leaving Vanya in the care of Klavdia, our old neighbour, I get to the apartment in good time, open a top-window to ventilate the place, and start dusting. Vanya and I washed the floor and the windows last September. The doorbell rings. I open the door to find the estate agent in a leather coat and the madam with brown hair from the cemetery.

"Good morning, Fyodor. This is Ms Sazonova," the agent announces with a professional smile. I feel an urge to slam the door in their faces. She ushers in my prospective tenant.

I don't know what life was like for Ms Sazonova before she met me, but when she sees me, she looks startled. She evidently isn't used to quite so many coincidences in such a short time, as indeed neither am I. And she doesn't yet know about the painting. I feel a momentary twinge of superiority at having experienced just that bit more mysticism.

"What are you doing here?" she demands by way of a greeting. Her lip is still swollen. She has powdered it.

"This is my apartment."

"Do you know each other?" The estate agent is flustered

and forgets to invite her prospect to put overshoes over her boots so as not to dirty the floor. How often people ask wholly unnecessary questions!

"Come in," I invite her. I could put both of them out, but recall Vanya's observation, "She is beautiful". Anyway, I need money.

Madam comes in, looking stressed, and examines the property. "Which way do the windows face?"

"Into the courtyard."

"I can see it's not on to the Champs Elysées. What direction does it face?"

"East. You get the sun in the morning."

"I don't see much sign of it."

"It's twelve-thirty."

She is clearly having some trouble focusing on the pros and cons of the apartment. Indeed, she is trying to decide whether or not to have anything to do with me. What advantage might there be for her in that? I can hear her cerebral microcircuits clanking.

"Are you letting it unfurnished?" she asks, by now less offensively.

"Yes."

"What about refurbishment?"

"You're welcome to do it for yourself."

Why should she care whether or not it is sunny? Why would she want it furnished? She is looking for an apartment to use as storage. I can't be bothered with this. We still have the rights to the grave to sort out. Although, I do need money. Now. Before she turned up, I only had completely unsuitable weirdos. If she wants it, she can have it.

"Well now, do you like it?" the agent enquires anxiously.

"I'll need to think about it," the woman replies ambiguously.

"I'll phone you," the agent tells me as she leaves. She's getting tired of me and my apartment.

I wait a few minutes, and then I leave too. In the courtyard I walk along the edge of the kerb, balancing. I've always liked that. You feel like you're tottering on the brink of a precipice. You're afraid you'll fall and that'll be the end of you, but when you do eventually lose your balance, there is no precipice, only the roadway.

A car slows down behind me. I always assume that, if a car pulls up alongside but just slightly behind, it's the cops. It's a puzzle what makes me so attractive to that category of the human species. I dress like any other citizen. I don't look like an immigrant or a refugee. Perhaps it's my expression they don't like. I've tested that theory. If you walk along briskly and look tense and anxious, they leave you alone. If, however, you stroll along in a leisurely sort of way, taking in everything around you, looking in the rubbish bins, they will check your ID. Perhaps, deep inside, I am a latent terrorist and the cops can sense it. These thoughts are interrupted by a familiar voice.

"Can I give you a lift?"

I turn round. Ms Sazonova sticks her head out of a dusty black Jeep. My heart misses a beat. I'm as scared as a schoolboy. What does she want? Has she decided to patch things up? She's sly. She wants to rent the apartment without going through the agency to avoid paying their commission. All sorts of silly ideas come into my head. She wants to find out more about the grave, on the quiet, one to one. Like, what plans do I have for ejecting her "dadda" from our family's hole in the ground. If I get in, I'll have to make polite conversation, she'll see through me, and realize I am a single dad down on his luck who can be fucked with impunity. I shouldn't get in, I mustn't... Oh, what the hell!

I'm already sitting on a soft car seat and the central locking system has clicked, locking the doors.

"Where are we going? And let's be friends... I'm Sonya."

"Fyodor." We shake hands and I tell her my address.

"Oof, what a cold hand!" Sonya laughs.

***

She is an edgy driver, constantly changing lanes.

"I thought you were the cops," I say to break the silence.

"What cops?"

"When you drove up. If you live in Moscow, sooner or later the cops check your ID. They have the greatest respect for me. They'll do anything for me. Once they even stopped a trolleybus."

"Wow!"

"I was sitting minding my own business, looking out the window when a cop car went by. There were such a lot of them crammed in it, like one big cop family coming in to paint the town red. They saw me and started yelling through a megaphone for the driver to stop the bus."

"Just like that? They saw you and stopped the trolleybus?" Sonya is unconvinced.

"Well, not quite. I had stuck my tongue out at them. They looked quite something all packed into their car. They hauled me out of the trolleybus and gave me a real going over!"

Sonya laughs. She seems to appreciate the story.

"What do you do?"

"Architecture, design." I see a blur in front of my eye and pull my eyelid forward with two fingers. Something sticks to them.

"You have great eyelashes," Sonya says as we approach

a dangerous bend without slowing down. I have to grab the handrail to avoid falling over on top of her.

Damn, I shouldn't have blurted out my profession. It would have been much better to remain mysterious. Perhaps I work in some secret service. Perhaps I have all sorts of levers of power in my grasp, and scary friends in black masks with false ID.

An old, dirty Lada with a Vladimir province registration number is trundling along, sagging under the weight of its load. The driver, some poor lost soul from far out of town, doesn't know which way to turn in the diabolical traffic flow. Sonya tries to overtake, moves in and out, this way and that, flashes her headlights, to no avail. We finally pass him. At the wheel is an ordinary Joe, his eyes goggling at the capital's traffic. She lowers the window and leans over me to shout, "Vladimir Province, welcome to Moscow!"

The man looks at us startled. Sonya chuckles. I smile, impressed by her breasts which, intentionally or not, she rubbed against me.

"You don't mind my chauvinism, do you?" I really hadn't expected her to be interested in my opinion. "Everybody's become so well-mannered nowadays."

"It's up to you." Personally, I haven't noticed everybody becoming well-mannered.

"I'm not into political correctness. Anyway, how are you tied up with that halfwit boy?"

"Look, don't call him a halfwit, okay?"

I've already got the virus which infects all parents of mentally backward children. I'm beginning to convince myself that Down syndrome kids are not half-witted but special children of God. Deep down, I think that's nonsense, but when people talk about Vanya I become stoutly defensive. Just like all my compatriots, who curse their homeland while they are in Russia, but turn into dyed-in-the-wool patriots abroad. Even herbivorous bespectacled intellectuals can demonstratively down a glass of vodka and threaten inoffensive Europeans with our Iskander missiles, or on Victory Day spit in the face of some fat burgher occupying the next room in a Turkish hotel. The parents of backward children, and I among them, are like provincials who rant on to inhabitants of the twin capitals that the air is cleaner in the countryside, there is less noise, and the food tastes better. The Muscovites and Petersburgers nod silently, smile indulgently, but decline to move out of their cities. The provincials for their part, contrary to their own declamations, often long to move a bit nearer to civilization.

"Look, don't tell me what I can or can't say," Sonya snaps back. Telling her what she can or can't say is not something I am planning to do.

"You know, just drop me off here," I say. "I guess this is my stop."

A screech of brakes almost sends me through the windscreen. I get out. I've had enough of these self-willed Moscow madams who are too used to ordering their juniors and housekeepers about. I walk away from the car, bump into someone, apologize. We have a serious property dispute and she's talking to me as if we've been married for ten years. I should never have got into the car.

"Hey, Fyodor, I'm sorry!" Sonya calls after me. She catches up, hazard lights flashing. "Stay cool. I won't talk like that again. Just don't punch me!" she says with satirical dismay, shielding herself from imaginary assault. "What's he got to do with you?"

"He…"

There and then, standing in the middle of the pavement, I tell her my whole life story. All about my parents, all about

Vanya. Sometimes that's how it is. You don't talk personal stuff with your friends but then, wham, all of a sudden you spill it all out to someone you've just come across by chance.

Sonya listens without interrupting, and says at the end, "Will you introduce me to Vanya? I'm interested now."

"Our apartment is a tip," I protest weakly.

***

Our staircase is considered very pretty. Ladies who love flowers have arranged pots of cacti, geraniums, and creeping vines on each landing. Aesthetically sensitive, they have hammered nails into the walls for calendars from the year before last, with pictures of birch trees and fluffy kittens. The elderly widow of one of the deputies of the last Soviet minister of defence has become very devout in recent years and plastered the walls of each flight of stairs with paper icons. I tried to phone Auntie Klavdia, who was looking after Vanya, but nobody answered. I really didn't want him spilling the beans to Sonya about the painting.

"Hello. I turn the phone off at night and forgot to turn it back on," she mumbled when I mentioned no one had answered. I brought her favourite chocolate cake. Our neighbour inspected Sonya approvingly, pleased to see that the Ovchinnikovs' son had finally brought a woman back to the parental home.

"What are you doing here?" Vanya asked Sonya sternly, but looking down at the floor.

"Vanya, this is Sonya. She is nice. Sonya this is Vanya."

Sonya shook Vanya's plump little hand with its stumpy fingers. I unlocked our door.

"Nice patch," Sonya said, casting a practised eye over the dusty lead crystal in the sideboard, the faded green wallpaper which retained its original colour only behind the cupboard, and the garish winter sunset painted by my grandfather's friend, a general who had taken up painting in retirement. With that, she plonked herself down in the sagging armchair covered in worn, rust-coloured velvet. The heirloom which had cost Vanya the role of Mercutio.

"My grandfather was a Hero of the Soviet Union."

"So you belong to 'a good family'," Sonya remarked, giving us an ironical wink. "My mum was a chemist and my dad an engineer. Only my grandfather took it into his head…"

Sonya stroked the black piano, running her hand over the crack in the lid. "Do you play?"

"I had lessons but didn't get anywhere. I can't do different things with my hands at the same time, and you're even supposed to use the pedals. Would you like some tea?"

No sooner had Sonya sat down on the bench in the kitchen than Vanya shooed her off and produced from the chest under the seat a dozen jars of jam which my parents had made in recent years. The jars had the year the jam was made written on them. Some bore stickers reading, "Respect. Obedience".

"What's that for?" Sonya asked.

"It's the kind of jam," I lied.

It was actually a leftover from my mother's battles with me. Stickers reading, "Respect. Obedience" were invariably affixed to the jars of homemade jam and apple juice from the dacha with which I was supplied every autumn. The intention was evidently to suffuse me from within with a becoming attitude towards my parents.

The table, already cluttered with stuff which didn't belong on it, was rapidly transformed into a storage facility for home-made jam. We had to strain our necks in order to see each other. Sonya giggled, I was embarrassed.

"Thank you, dear Vanya," Sonya said, washing a saucer for the jam. "The water doesn't seem to be draining properly." A pool of dirty water stagnated in the sink.

After rapidly assessing the situation, Vanya announced, "A blockage again". He sounded like a hands-on apartment owner. "Dad, where's the plunger?" He was displaying his peacock tail for the benefit of our lady guest.

"It's in the bathroom."

Vanya found the plunger and loud squishing noises came from the sink as he made short work of the obstruction. Simultaneously, he related, "The pipes are past it and this entire residential block hasn't been properly maintained. Mayor Luzhkov allocated the funds, but they were stolen."

"Who stole them?"

"The manager! He bought himself a Hyundai," Vanya continued confidently. "We were away at the dacha."

"I imagine the dacha too came from your grandfather?"

I should not have brought her back here. It was really stupid. Any minute now, Vanya will blurt everything out and we'll be thrown out of our own grave.

"From grandfather. It's very good. It has a stove, radiators, and a toilet," Vanya counted off its amenities on his fingers, swelling with pride. "Our neighbour Victor Timofeyich says it's really sound."

"Brilliant!" Sonya said admiringly.

"That's just what our neighbour thinks," I elaborated. "Our dacha is nothing special by today's standards. My grandfather was a general, he taught at the academy. His students are powerful people nowadays," I added, giving Sonya a meaningful look.

Vanya offered her some apple jelly.

"Oh, look," she said. "It's got flies in it!"

We looked into the piece of jelly wobbling on her spoon

and, sure enough, as if set in amber, it had a couple of small insects in it.

"Let's open a different jar," I suggested.

"It's nothing. I'll just dissolve the jam in the tea, they'll float to the surface, and I'll pick them out," Sonya said.

A bell rang, making me jump. Sonya pulled a mobile phone out of her handbag. "Hello... Fine... Guess who I'm visiting!... Who we now share a grave with... Yes... Come over, I'll tell…" She covered the phone with her hand and turned to Vanya and me. "Can my sister come round? Masha. You saw her at the cemetery."

"Yes, of course, delighted." Now we're going to have her sister to cope with as well. "Come on over." Sonya dictated the address.

"I'm going to have a phone soon too," Vanya said importantly, wriggling about on his chair.

"Wow! Will you give me your number?"

"Sure!" Vanya blushed and clamped his little fists between his knees. "Dad is going to buy me the very best one which can download music from the TV. I will download music and the phone will play it," Vanya explained, adding gratuitously, "It's my birthday soon!"

"Your birthday! When? How old will you be?"

"It is my birthday right after Dad's, on 27 December. I will be sixteen years old," he said, meticulously pronouncing this tirade. Vanya looked at me as if I were a teacher to whom he had just read a poem he had memorized.

"You've given away all our family secrets," I joked.

"So you both have birthdays soon! Will you invite me?"

"Certainly we will," I say, beginning to tire of her persistence.

"They didn't float up," Sonya remembered as she drank up the last of her tea.

"Did you swallow them?" Vanya asked in alarm. Leaning back on the bench, Sonya surveyed the kitchen.

"What artistic re-decoration! Did you do it yourselves?"

"Yes." A few years ago, our neighbours upstairs caused a flood. That was the fault of the pipes too. The water wasn't draining properly. My parents would just have gone on living with the peeling paint hanging in shreds from the ceiling, but I offered to do the re-decoration for them. I thought it would be an interesting experience. Vanya was already quite big, and together we scraped off the old paint and plaster. We stripped away everything that wasn't firmly attached. Then I bought a bucket of paint, some colourants, mixed a couple of hues in a trough, and started painting the ceiling.

Standing on the stepladder, Vanya had a sudden insight. The whole ceiling looked to him like the map of a fantastic world. My father was teaching him geography and he knew what maps looked like. The grey areas, where the plaster and old paint had been stripped down to the underlying concrete, were the oceans. The white areas, where the plaster had not yielded to the stripping knife or hammer, were the islands and continents. The outlines of land and sea were clearly visible.

We promptly made up a story that here, on the kitchen ceiling, we had discovered a mysterious world with its own Europes, Americas, and Asias; with high mountains and deep gorges; with volcanoes, cities and rivers. I hazarded a guess that this was the world in which the Land of Miracle Yogurt was located. Vanya had just seen the adverts for Miracle Yogurt for the first time and was constantly asking everyone where that country was.

"Here it is," I said, pointing to the largest area of plaster.

"Who lives there?" he asked, enchanted.

"The people who live there are quite different. Not like

us…" I was running out of ideas, and suddenly blurted out without thinking, "The people who live there are like you."

Vanya was only ten or eleven, but he already knew he was different from other people. The news had an effect which was entirely unexpected. Vanya forbade any further painting. "That is my country! The Land of Miracle Yogurt!" he sang in a strange echo of the advert. "I want to see it!"

After several unsuccessful attempts to dissuade him, like claiming the map needed to be camouflaged, we accepted defeat. The ceiling was left unpainted. To this day, Vanya loves looking at it. His fairy-tale world has generated many new stories, which he makes up himself. Now he told Sonya all the details.

"How do you get there?" she asked. "I would like to see this country. I'm tired of Thailand."

Vanya replied without hesitation, "You can only go to this country after you die. But they don't let everybody in, only people like me. But I'll be able to invite you to visit."

"Do, please, invite me! I'll definitely come! But right now I am desperately hungry. Guys, do you think we should order a pizza?"

"We don't need a pizza!" Vanya protested, producing from the refrigerator a piece of meat we bought yesterday. Our last rations.

"Dad, let's cook the meat!"

"What a great idea! We should stop stuffing ourselves with junk food!" Sonya concurred enthusiastically. I was less happy. We had nothing to eat, and Vanya was proposing to feed what little was left to outsiders. Nevertheless, saving face had to take priority.

"Then give it a wash and look for a roasting bag. You remember, we bought some."

"Bag, ha-ha-ha! Roasting bag!" Vanya fooled around,

overexcited by the presence of a beautiful young woman. Just like me when I was a kid. I remember going on a bus with my parents. There were two schoolgirls sitting opposite. To me, they seemed to be grown-up, beautiful ladies. I started pulling faces, squirming around, fidgeting, doing everything I could to attract their attention. But then my father went and told me to behave properly in front of other people. I felt as if I'd been shot down in mid-flight. I burrowed into my mother's side and wailed. Why did my father have to humiliate me in front of the schoolgirls?

"What does Masha do?"

"Sweet fuck-all."

Vanya, shoving the meat into the bag, stood stock still. What would he have to say to that?

"It's not good to swear. It spoils your karma." Good for him: no double standards!

"How do you know? "Sonya asked unabashed.

"The angel told me."

She had underestimated her opponent.

"Do you talk to angels?" she asked, unable to conceal her surprise.

"My mum taught me how to," Vanya answered proudly.

"My mother was into that sort of stuff. Just out of boredom." All we needed now was for Sonya to decide we were nuts. Although, that might scare her a bit. She might decide it was best not to get on the wrong side of us. We might just do her in, spend some time in the loony bin, and then get back out.

"I won't swear any more then, if the angel says you mustn't. In other words, Masha doesn't do anything. Sometimes she gives French lessons. Her mother is French, an art historian who came to the Soviet Union for a seminar and our dad was right in there. So Masha is actually Maria-

Letizia-Geneviève. It's only in Russia she is Masha. She lives here some of the time and then in Paris. While she's here, mother rents her an apartment at Patriarch Ponds."

Vanya put in the roasting tin and asked me to light the gas. While we were waiting for Masha, we carried on chatting. It sometimes happens that in a single day more things happen than usually occur in six months. It's as if whoever manages our destinies comes to the end of his shift and, before handing over to the next administrator, lavishly shakes out all the events he hasn't managed to find a place for earlier.

"We are almost family now. Brothers and sisters through a grave. Tell me, what do you do for a living?" I asked Sonya.

"My mother is a translator, my father was an artist…"

At the word "artist" Vanya gave me such an eloquent look that Sonya noticed. I waved dismissively and gave Vanya the exact same look, as if it was a kind of joke between us.

"Masha and I have the same father. He abandoned my mother and me when I was five years old. Masha had already been born." Sonya took a drag on her cigarette.

"Are you an artist, too?" Vanya broke in.

"No. I deal in other people's masterpieces. I sell European paintings to our compatriots, who are clueless about painting. I have a clever lad in Holland, a former fellow student of mine. He goes round the flea markets buying up old landscapes and sends them to me by train. I pass them off here as little-known Western masterpieces."

"Is business good?"

"The wives of middle-ranking businessmen cheerfully pay ten or twenty thousand Euros for things I pick up for five hundred. I steer clear of really rich people. They have their own art experts. My customers are people with a million or two who want to dabble in the aristocratic pastime of collecting art."

For the ten years of my working career I've tried only to create beautiful interiors, fighting over every detail, trying to talk round clients and builders, and refusing to touch barbaric re-development of old buildings. That's why I never got rich. Here is quite a different family, with dadda churning out vulgar smut and his cynical daughter palming idiots off with second-rate paintings she claims are old masters. To view it more charitably, Sazonov and Sonya give people what they deserve, stuff they won't choke on. You can't feed gammon to a one-year-old baby.

Nearby something popped. "What's that?" Vanya jumped up, nervously licking his lips. I dropped a teaspoon and it clattered treacherously onto the saucer.

"The meat!" Sonya twigged. Vanya immediately grabbed the oven door handle and leapt back with a yell. The old stove gets very hot. I rushed around looking for oven gloves while Vanya blew on his fingers. Sonya calmly took a towel, opened the oven, and pulled out the reluctant roasting tin with a harsh grating sound.

Dense smoke snaked out, stinging our eyes. There was a smell of burning rubber, like during some African rebellion when insurgents are setting fire to tyres.

"Yuck!" The meat, with the molten remains of the roasting bag clinging to it, was ablaze.

"Useless roasting bag!" Vanya exclaimed. I filled a glass with water and threw it over the flaming "heat-resistant" bag. The kitchen was plunged into a dense, evil-smelling fog which made us cough and rub our smarting eyes. The doorbell rang.

***

In the doorway stood Maria-Letizia-Geneviève, a straight-haired blonde just a little taller and slimmer than Sonya. She resembled a jointed wooden doll, thin, straight, and angular. Her bright blue eyes had a dreamy look. A hazel fleck showed in her right eye, like a fragment of broken beer bottle. Masha gave the impression of having just got out of bed. The right-hand corner of her mouth seemed to have been rubbed out with an eraser. At first you thought you were imagining it, but then realized it was for real. It made her symmetrical face looked slightly skewed.

"Have you set their house on fire?" Masha asked Sonya. "The concierge downstairs is wondering whether to call the fire brigade."

"The roasting bag was defective," Vanya explained coyly, before hiding behind my back, blushing furiously.

"Where is the kitchen? Oh, hello!" Masha pecked us both twice on the cheek in the French manner.

Directness was the only obvious quality the sisters shared. They didn't pull their punches and used bad language, but they were not looking down on Vanya as something weird, or gazing at him with that expression of fake compassion.

Vanya was shocked by the kisses. He had never been kissed by a girl before. For a few moments, he stood dumbstruck, then bowed ceremoniously, but Masha with Sonya in tow had already rushed through to the kitchen.

"Oh, I see our new friends are the great chefs," Masha exclaimed, picking with a fork at the congealed crust of burnt polythene stuck to the meat.

"It looks like a murdered extraterrestrial. Let me see the packaging of this 'bag' of yours."

We rummaged guiltily in the drawer of the sideboard

and handed her the box. Masha read out, "'For use in a microwave oven'! What geniuses! You have to read to the end of the instructions!"

"But we don't have a microwave!" Vanya explained.

Contrary to expectation, the meat was cooked perfectly. Not overcooked, not red. The occasional scrap of melted polythene was neither here nor there. Dissecting it into four equal pieces, I served it up.

"When are you going to give us our grave back?" Vanya suddenly asked with his mouth full. Sonya put down her knife and fork. Masha sighed.

"Vanya, let's talk about this after the meal," I began.

"We can talk about it now. It's high time," Sonya intervened. "We understand it's really not very nice…"

"Sonya, it is horrible. This is the sort of thing which can happen only in Russia!" Masha added quickly.

"You see, my father specially wanted to be buried in that cemetery. The artist Surikov and the poet Sergey Yesenin are buried there. We asked at the funeral parlour whether there were any plots available and they said it could be arranged. We didn't go into the details. We were too upset."

"We don't need to rush you. We're not in any hurry to use the grave, eh, Vanya?" I winked at my son but he didn't see the joke.

"Why aren't we in a hurry?" he asked.

"Please don't worry. We'll demand a different plot, and pay you compensation," Sonya concluded.

"You are going to dig Dadda up?" Masha enquired.

"Dadda is lying in someone else's place. He did that often enough when he was alive!" Sonya giggled. Masha smiled wanly. "Moving over a bit will do him no harm now."

I wondered whether as a boy young Gosha Sazonov, who grew up to become the artist "Georges Sazonoff", could have imagined that just before he died his last picture would be stolen by a boy with Down syndrome, while his body would be shoved into a grave belonging to the thief's family, who would insist that he be re-buried.

"Come and see me in the theatre!" Vanya invited all present.

"In the theatre?"

"I am acting in a play!" My pumpkin writhed proudly from side to side. He even began to show off some dance steps. The sisters turned to me questioningly.

"Well, uh... it's not really a theatre, just a basement with a small stage... Vanya is acting in a play... um, a small role…"

"I am playing Mercutio!"

I decided not to remind him he had been deprived of that role.

"Wow!" the sisters shrieked, and rushed to tickle and hug Vanya.

"You're an actor as well!"

Vanya squealed with laughter.

"And what is the play!" Sonya asked.

"Sonya, you disgrace our family!" Masha retorted.

"What? Oh, yes, of course, er, *Hamlet*? Just kidding! And you are playing Mercutio?"

"Yes…" Vanya looked at me, suddenly perplexed. He had remembered.

"Vanya is trying out a different role at the moment," I said, riding to the rescue. "Which?"

"He is going to welcome the spectators and read the final monologue."

"And why not Mercutio?" Sonya asked with undue curiosity. Masha coughed, realizing that further probing was unwelcome.

"Well, there's Kirill, and his mum bought them furniture, so they gave Mercutio to him."

"They took the role away from you because of some furniture?"

"Oh, it wasn't exactly…" I intervened.

"Well, actually, yes." Vanya hung his head.

"We bring them this armchair every time, but they want permanent props, new… Anyway, there's this lady on the parents' committee, and she negotiated with them…"

"When is the performance?"

"The day after tomorrow at eight. It's the first show this season. We'll take them the chair anyway."

"It's the premiere!" Vanya announced solemnly.

"I love premieres!" Masha exclaimed, clasping her hands together.

"And how are you going to get that monstrosity there? It's that chair in the living room we're talking about?" Sonya asked very practically.

"We'll hire a van."

"I'll take you."

Vanya disappeared and returned with a brass bugle.

"Look at that!" Sonya exclaimed admiringly. "May I blow it?"

"Certainly," Vanya said, like the maiden in a conservative family assenting to her fiancé's touching her hand. Sonya produced a long, tuneless hoot.

"Let me show you!" Vanya tore the bugle from Sonya's hands and produced a number of noises even more cacophonous. The sisters clapped their hands. Vanya was in his element now, and did what I had most feared.

"Would you like me to show you my collection?"

"Vanya, I really don't think the girls want to see that."

"Why not? It's really interesting!"

Vanya led our guests through while I trailed after him, at a loss as to how to prevent the painting from being displayed. I took a cup from the table and had a sip as I walked past. It went down the wrong way. Coughing, wheezing, gasping for air, I flailed my arms, my eyes rolling. Vanya scampered over and started thumping me on the back. I wiped away tears.

Boom! Boom! Boom! The clock in the living room chimed.

"What's the time?" Everybody seemed to wake up.

"Eleven!" I croaked. I had never before told anyone the time with such relief.

"Oh dear, we've overstayed! I have an early meeting tomorrow, and I expect it's time for you to get to bed. Thank you for dinner!"

***

After the sisters' visit, I viewed the apartment through their eyes. It wasn't just a shambles, it was an indescribable rubbish tip. There were clumps of dust under the cupboards. I set about cleaning the place, beginning with the bedroom.

I dismantled my parents' bed. From under the mattress, like scuttling cockroaches, portraits of faith healer Semenkov rained down. They were supposed to have curative powers. Mum believed that with their aid she would make Vanya the same as everybody else. Semenkov was a balding man who had let his hair grow long over his collar. You were supposed to place his glossy photograph under your mattress and to wear it under your clothing. Mum literally covered herself and Vanya with his portraits. The more photos you used, the more potent the healing effect. To protect the photos from wear and tear, she placed them in transparent plastic sleeves. When she or Vanya made the slightest movement, they rustled like purchases in a supermarket.

I gathered up the photos and hadn't the heart to throw them out. I decided to put them up in the top cupboard. Bringing out the stepladder, covered in paint from when we were re-decorating, I opened the top cupboard door. I breathed in the smell of old cloth, leather, and wood and surveyed piles of packages, a folding chess board with its varnish peeling and the chess pieces rattling inside, a yellowed roll of floral wallpaper.

And here was the small case containing my grandfather's awards: the Order of Lenin, the Order of the Red Star, the star of Hero of the Soviet Union. I preferred the Red Star to the others, with its enamel, five-pointed star the colour of stewed cherries and the grey soldier in the middle. The Orders were fixed to a black velvet cushion, which was placed on my grandfather's chest during his funeral. After that, the cushion was hidden away in this case and my grandfather was hidden away in the ground.

I remembered him telling me how he earned that Red Star. He spoke about it only once, shortly before he died. During the war, he was the commanding officer of a unit of engineers. In the winter of 1943, he was ordered to bridge a river in a single night. The Germans' bombardment was relentless. The river became a mush of churning frigid water and crushed ice, a Russian Mojito cocktail. My grandfather was told that if there was a bridge in the morning he would be put up for an award; if there wasn't, he would be shot. Grandpa thought for a moment and asked HQ for two things: ten barrels of vodka and a sackful of medals. They gave him only half the amount of vodka but didn't stint on the medals.

My grandfather gave the sappers their orders and awarded them their medals in advance. Each got three or four Orders and several medals. Other soldiers didn't earn that many in the entire course of the war. Then they advanced into the icy water and the bombardment. In the morning, the barrels were empty and Soviet tanks were thundering across the new bridge. Nearly all the sappers were dead. My grandfather lost his left arm.

I recently sold a German bronze chandelier, a war trophy, to an antique shop. There were a lot of military awards in the window: Red Stars, Orders of Lenin, Iron Crosses with oak leaves, insignia for the advance in the Kuban. After just sixty years, these pretty pieces of metal, which lured so many young men into the next world, are jumbled together in an antique shop. Medals awarded to mortal enemies now lie peacefully side by side with Soviet medals in a collector's case.

A package containing squares of paper for notes came crashing down. My mother economically re-used empty cartons. Dad cut them into neat squares. They were used for shopping lists or for issuing guidance to me. For some reason, even used squares had been kept.

I bent down to gather them all up when another package, full of plastic sour cream containers, fell out. They were handy for storing food. If my parents had lived in Europe, the Greens would have given them an award for their contribution to recycling. Finally, a bag containing balls of old wool fell on my head. A few rolled down the corridor, smelling of mothballs and the 1980s. I once helped my grandmother unravel a cardigan and wind one of these balls. She loved unraveling old clothes but never got round to knitting anything new. As I was shoving the wool back, my hand felt a parcel tied with string. I pulled it out, unwrapped the newspaper, and found a large wad of outdated hundred-ruble notes and some government bond certificates.

In her last years, Grandma would get our names wrong and was constantly hiding money. She would insert it in books or put it under a mattress. She would hide it very effectively, and then forget where she had put it. Every time it ended in a family quarrel. Grandma accused my mother of stealing her savings and bonds, Dad would stand up for my mother, Mum would argue with Grandma, my father would stand up for Grandma, and so on. Finally, he would slam the door and flee to the courtyard. That sort of thing happened regularly once a month, after Grandma received her pension. The last time her savings disappeared was about a year before she died, in 1990. The money was never found. My parents were seriously upset because Grandma had saved up around three thousand Soviet rubles. Their turn to buy a car had come up and they wanted to sell the old Zhiguli and get a new one. How grandmother got up to the ceiling cupboard at her age I can't imagine.

Some balls of wool unwound and I wound them up again. You could make any of them into a hat. When you tired of the hat, you could unravel it and knit a sweater. If the sweater went out of fashion, you could make a scarf. When the scarf showed signs of wear you could make socks or anything you fancied. The essence does not change, only the form. Everything gets wound into a ball: thought, friendships, history, destiny. Everything starts with a single stitch, the end of a piece of wool, and everything goes back to that first stitch.

So, this is my inheritance. A pile of old junk and a mentally backward teenager. My life flashes past before my eyes. I quarrel with my parents over those cardboard squares for notes instead of just having a neat notebook. As a teenager, I thought how cool it would be if my parents died in an accident and I could sort out the apartment. I was ashamed of the unfashionable way they dressed, and how old they were. I wished my parents were younger, like those of most of the kids in the courtyard. I wished my mother was a dressed-up painted doll and my father swaggering and rich, not a retired Soviet official with only small change jingling in his pockets. I wanted our apartment to be full of modern furniture, the old oak window frames to be PVC, to buy food in supermarkets where they only accepted foreign currency. I thought I would soon be in the big time. Then I would show them all! Now here I am, the victor, the proud owner of this apartment.

I am a copy of my father, a dismally bad careerist. I could already have had my own interior design firm, like many of my classmates. I would have young guys working for me. Why didn't I just take the step of leaving Vanya with that nurse? Okay, so he would have been asleep, what's so terrible about that! I would have been making money and socializing with the wives of my clients.

I threw down a ball of wool, flung those cardboard squares covered in writing up in the air, the plastic containers, Grandma's banknotes. They covered the corridor like a scattered pack of cards. Vanya peeped anxiously out of his (my) room. He is the croupier in the casino of destiny, and the money is cards I throw down in a vain attempt to outplay my destiny.

***

The next evening, after I'd got Vanya ready for the theatre, I went at the last moment to take a shower. I had to wait a few minutes for the water to come to a reasonable temperature. When we turn on the hot water tap, cold water comes out. It only warms up after a while and, if you are lucky, eventually becomes hot.

I emerged from the bathroom to find Sonya sitting in the kitchen in evening dress. "How was your shower?" She was earlier than expected. I had to go by in just my underpants.

"Got anything to drink?" Sonya asked, detaining me.

"To drink?" I concentrated, pulling in my stomach and trying to adopt a more flattering pose while still appearing casual.

"We've got the mushroom!" Vanya contributed.

"What?"

"The mushroom! The mushroom!" Vanya was already reaching into the sideboard and hauling out a three-litre jar of yellow liquid, on the surface of which floated a substance which combined the appearance of a sponge, meat, and the cap of a giant mushroom. This was "the mushroom", a strange fermentation culture which produced a fizzy sweet-and-sour beverage.

"God Almighty, what's that?"

"It is a medicinal mushroom, which was... was known more than…" Vanya started in on his memorized lecture but lost the thread, forgetting quite when the mushroom had been known.

"In ancient China. Perhaps you'd just like some water?" I rounded off his speech, trying to switch Sonya's attention to a different subject, but it was too late.

"A mushroom! My mother had one just like it!" Sonya clucked. "We must drink some mushroom!"

"May it bring you good health!" Vanya carefully filled a glass. "I wash it every week."

Soviet housewives loved this fungus. They propagated it, invented new additives, divided and shared it with their friends, fed it sugar, washed and pampered it in every way possible, like an old, wise, respected member of the family. Sonya sipped tentatively.

"Fantastic, guys! I'm so glad we met! Mushroom! Where else would I ever have come across it!" She drained the glass and asked for more. Vanya happily obliged.

"To think, my mother threw ours out!"

"Everybody did. I don't know how it's survived with us," I replied, as if realizing for the first time that we had it.

In the 1990s, the mushroom lost its status. Fickle Soviet wives were immediately unfaithful and took up with Coca-Cola and Sprite, forgetting all about its antiquity and medicinal properties. First they started neglecting the mushroom in its three-litre jar, drinking what remained of the liquid for old times' sake, but then they just threw the fungus in the trash. Yesterday's star lay there in rubbish bins among the eggshells, chicken bones, and soggy newspapers, which people at the time used for lining waste bins. The mushrooms looked like beached jellyfish.

Only a few women stayed faithful to their mushroom, and my mother was one of them. Her mushroom saw out the collapse of the Soviet Union, Yeltsin's assault on the republican government's White House, the Moscow hurricane, and the 1998 currency default, the war in Chechnya, the watery deaths in the submarine Kursk, and the death of its patron. I'm slightly embarrassed by the mushroom, but deep in my heart recognize it is a living thing. Vanya takes care of it and treats it like a god of the hearth.

Sonya examined its layered, fleshy structure. "It's so soft, and slippery, and round. If I was a man, I'd most definitely fuck it. Have you tried?"

"We... we... no," I said, cringing at the very thought of sex with a fungus. Vanya said nothing and looked terribly confused, so that for a moment I even thought... But no, surely not.

"God, how I'd fuck it! I sometimes really regret not having a prick," Sonya elaborated, sipping from the glass and casting a glance in my direction. All we needed was for

Vanya to be instructed in these matters by our new friend.
I could imagine him even starting furtively to fuck the
mushroom. The poor thing would have cause then to envy
its brothers their fate of drying out among the trash twenty
years ago.

"What haven't you got?" Vanya asked.

"We need to leave soon! Vanya, have you got
everything?"

"Yes."

I hotfoot it to my room to finally get dressed. Sonya
follows close on my heels with her glass, considering the
pros and cons of screwing a fungus.

"Of course, it's clammy, but it can't answer back and
you aren't going to catch anything from it! It might grow
into a half-person half-fungus. Perhaps that's been done long
ago and just kept secret! I've seen a lot of people who look
like this poppet. Their faces were just the same! And what
if it's from an extraterrestrial civilization?" Sonya stopped a
few steps behind me for a moment. "Why didn't that occur
to me before! It is completely obvious that the mushroom is
an alien!"

While she was in the corridor enraptured by this insight,
I managed to pull on my jeans. "Have you never wanted to
fuck an alien?" She came very close and looked into my
eyes. We were standing really very close to each other. Too
close. And I was half naked.

"It never occurred to me. Vanya, are you ready?" I
shouted over her shoulder, perhaps a bit too loudly. Vanya
appeared instantly at the door, as if he might have been
eavesdropping.

"Yes. You asked already."

"It's time to load up, or we'll be late."

***

Grunting, snagging the door handles and banging into the doors jambs, I lugged the armchair out to the lift and locked the apartment. I don't let Vanya carry heavy loads because of his heart. We squeezed our old German loot into the narrow Russian elevator, which meant we had to press back the plush "ears" sticking out of the chair's back.

"You should have bought another one long ago and given this one to the theatre," Sonya volunteered, seeing my efforts.

"I wouldn't want another one. This one really inspires me," Vanya said, flatly rejecting the suggestion.

"Perhaps the other one would inspire you even more."

"No, it wouldn't."

To my relief, the chair fitted in the back of Sonya's Jeep. We got into the rear seats and she drove out on to the bridge.

"Is it antique?" My question was about an icon which I found beside me under a pile of magazines.

Sonya looked back in the mirror.

"Ah, I was looking for that. No, it's modern work, but good quality. St Sergius of Radonezh. Icons are the most robust segment of the art market. It's difficult to establish the age of an icon. Smart artists buy old boards and paint on them. You can really fox the experts. I'm sure you must be able to paint."

"I suppose so."

"I have an ex-member of the Artists' Union working for me. He used to knock out Lenins but now he does icons. They sell very well. If you don't want to starve in your old age, paint some icons now and start selling them in thirty years' time."

"Thanks for the tip."

Vanya and I look closely at the countenance of the

Russian saint, painted by an artist formerly specializing in the leader of the world proletariat. I like it. The colours are simple but rich. A wise old man looks back at us. He knows everything, past and future. Although he does have a squint a bit like Lenin's, and his beard is also a bit goatee.

***

When we arrive at the basement theatre, we place the armchair centre stage. Vanya changes into his costume and takes up position front of house, ready to welcome the audience. His page's outfit has been put together out of costumes my mother had sewn for him. He has a long velvet coat the colour of watermelon flesh, an orange shirt front, and black trousers. He bows gallantly and says ceremoniously, "Good evening! Welcome!" and invites people to be seated. Masha appears. Relatives of the other actors look our way with curiosity, even a certain envy. The sisters look out of place, like inhabitants of a different, unattainable world of prosperity and fun.

We are seated on a bench in the third and last row. In this production, the first two rows are considered high-risk. You are likely to get a punch in the face from a Romeo gesticulating too energetically, or to take a saliva shower as Juliet sprays the public with her declaration of love. The audience are mainly the mothers and grandmothers of the Down syndrome cast. The dads have usually dumped such families. Also present are people professionally involved with the mentally handicapped: psychologists, teachers, people working for charities. From the little room next to the stage come loud whispers and tapping sounds as last-minute preparations are made.

Finally, the lights go down and a spot is illuminated into which the sensual-looking director steps. The music starts a little late because Tybalt's grandmother is not yet entirely au fait with the control panel. With extravagant gestures and making sheep's eyes at the audience, the director very expressively tells the expectant audience the names of the characters in the play and the sequence of events. The production does not slavishly follow Shakespeare. The director explains this as due to the fact that there are many ways of reading the text. In his way, everything revolves not around the star-crossed love between two young hearts, but around the mystical transmigration of souls. Why the director has violated the underlying principle of drama by revealing the plot at the outset becomes clear with Romeo's first lines.

"Oo-ow-o...," he says, assuming a highly meaningful and solemn expression. I imagine the impression that "Oo-ow-o" must have made on the sisters. They were expecting a performance, strange, unpredictable, but nevertheless a play with more or less comprehensible words. Here, instead of words, they are hearing mumbled half-words. Many Downs speak unclearly. Their tongues are too big, which makes it difficult for them to articulate sounds. They even out all the detail, the humps and angles and idiosyncrasy of the words and turn them into ill-defined blank cartridges. They sound the way your own words would sound if you just opened your mouth and tried to pronounce them without using your tongue or lips. They are like unpainted nesting dolls.

Some of the actors shout where they ought to whisper, others forget their words. The nurse delivers her lines exhaling loudly after every word, as if lifting a heavy weight, while Juliet and Count Paris prompt her and give her advice. Don't be frightened, they say, try to remember the words, speak with expression. The nurse nods acknowledgment, promising not to spoil things.

I feel very awkward about the sisters' coming, personally responsible for every lapse on the stage. I hold my breath, mentally urging the Downs not to give up. When I am in an embarrassing situation, I just want to become very small and disappear. Luckily, I've got someone's mother sitting in front of me wearing an immense pink beret. She has it pulled down over the back of her head and it is like a large pancake in front of my nose. Anybody else might be upset to have the stage obscured by such large-calibre headgear, but I'm only too glad to hide behind it. I scrutinize the gaps in the parquet, my neighbours' shoes.

Kirill, who is playing Mercutio, drips hot wax from a candle, burns his hand, and all but wrecks the whole play. The director manages to persuade him not to leave the stage prematurely, but Kirill is a reluctant actor from then on, constantly blowing on his burn. As a result, the fatal duel is a disaster, and the phrase, "A plague on both your houses", sounds petty and querulous rather than prophetic. I am vindictively pleased. That'll teach you how not to choose people for roles. My Vanya would never have made such a fuss about a minor burn, and his diction is better, and he knows the part.

The director's cue, "Enter Juliet", for a long time produces no actress, and only after he has vanished into the room next to the stage to see what has happened does it transpire that she has gone to the toilet accompanied by her grandmother. While we wait, Tybalt's grandmother abandons the control panel to give her grandson a cake.

Juliet, a toothy girl in spectacles, doesn't let us down, singing to Romeo, "I'll make you so lonely, baby, you could die". Their declaration of love is made in our armchair. Juliet sits on the armrest while Romeo sprawls on the seat.

"I'll make you so lonely, baby, you could die!" Juliet

booms in an alluring, throaty contralto. Romeo, a fat boy who keeps looking at his left shoulder, yells in a fit of bravado, "Yeah, baby! Come on!" earning himself a storm of applause.

Realizing he is on to something, Romeo starts egging Juliet on with more exclamations along the lines of, "Yeah, baby!" She sings her song over and over again, each time more suggestively, and kicks up her legs, unmindful of her short skirt. The scene stretches out to five minutes or so, and the audience, touched, claps appreciatively.

At the end, Tybalt's grandmother kills the lights and the whole company on stage is covered with a black cloth. The director's vision was that, concealed by the cloth, the actors should invisibly leave the darkened stage. No such luck. They immediately forget their obligations to the audience and begin to play tents. Their whispering and blundering about causes a break in the proceedings and the director has to jump up on to the stage and shepherd his wards to the side door. There is a second hitch when Romeo, who is leading the way, cannot at first find the door, or then the handle he needs to pull towards himself. This causes those coming behind to bump into those in front, causing a minor crush and a certain amount of ill-feeling. The vigilant director takes control of the situation, opens the door, and gently but forcefully pushes the actors off stage.

Vanya emerges into a ray of light, moves one leg behind the other, and carefully and expressively begins, "Never was a story of more woe…" At that, my mobile phone rings. I was sure I'd left it in my jacket in the cloakroom. It shrills again.

"Never was a story of more woe / Than this of…"

The ringtone seems to get longer and louder. I frantically turn out the pockets of my jeans, my sweatshirt, my back pockets. Some coins fall out and roll over the floor in the deadly silence, sounding like a court verdict. Coins, crumpled banknotes, bits of card with notes written on them... "Trr-ing! Trrrr-ing!!" A void expands around me. Everyone turns, annihilating me with their withering glances. "Trrrrr-ing!!!!" Where is the goddam phone?

"That was my only line!" Taken by surprise, I look up abruptly. Vanya is leaning over the chair in front of me. The spectators in the first two rows have moved apart. "Yes... I'm sorry... Oh!" I finally fish out the phone, press all the buttons at once without looking, and silence it. "I'm sorry."

The director runs on to the stage and finishes the epilogue. What have I done! Vanya doesn't come out for the final bow. We run to the room at the side of the stage, Masha bearing a bouquet of purple tulips she has kept hidden in paper. Needless to say, nobody has brought flowers for any of the other actors. Vanya is mumbling something under his breath and toying with his hands.

"Vanya, forgive me, please." I look into his eyes. "I thought the phone was in my jacket. I forgot." Vanya keeps his head down like a recalcitrant bullock. "It was the estate agent. Perhaps we've got a taker. We'll let the apartment and have some money!" I stop short. Sonya is standing next to me and arguably she is already a taker.

"These are for you," Masha says, holding out the bouquet. "You were wonderful!"

The director looks in the door. Sonya, without a moment's hesitation, says, "Your theatre collective's professionalism and ensemble acting are simply amazing!"

"Eet was a magneeficent prodooction, and, even in Paree, ay more... 'ow you say in Russian?... oreeginal interpretation I 'ave nevair seen," Masha enthuses with an exaggerated French accent.

"The spirit of equality and creativity is truly admirable!"

The director proves unable to resist this onslaught, and hearing that the sisters are "Vanya's cousins", promises to resolve the misunderstanding over the role of Mercutio. At this moment, Kirill arrives and moves in on Sonya.

"Who are you? You are beautiful!"

"Thank you. So are you," Sonya replies.

"Kirill, these are our visitors," the director says in the icy tone of a lady drinking tea with relatives unexpectedly up from the country when her rowdy, drunken husband bursts in.

"I've dreamed of you," Kirill continues. It's a pity he couldn't have equaled this performance on stage. "Can I hold your hand?"

Before Sonya can answer, he's grabbed her round the waist. Sonya screams and begins fighting the amorous Kirill off. He paws her with unexpected purposefulness. The director, instead of coming to her aid, starts apologizing.

"Oh, I am sorry, I am so sorry!"

The contretemps is resolved as quickly as it began. Kirill's grandmother charges in and drags her protesting grandson off by the collar.

"Am I going to play Mercutio again?" Vanya asks.

"M-m-m, perhaps, perhaps…" the director mumbles.

***

"Let's celebrate!" Masha suggests, getting into the car.

"Yes, yes!" Vanya concurs.

"Let's go to your dacha! Isn't it fairly near here?" Sonya asks.

"Come on, Dad!"

I need somehow to atone for that phone call during his performance. "Okay, let's go."

I wonder how long it will take for our new friends to get bored with us. When will they lose interest in playing the role of liberal-minded sympathizers and fade away? Vanya will miss them, wear me down, fall ill.

"Then let's go and buy wine, food and toothbrushes!" Sonya commands. Toothbrushes? Are they planning on staying the night?

Having got the armchair loaded back into the car, we drive to the supermarket and stock up with supplies. We buy a string of sausages specially for Vanya who has suddenly decided not to eat meat any more because he is sorry for the animals. He doesn't associate sausages with animals. Besides, he likes the fact that they hang like a garland. While we are sitting in the back seat, he winds the sausages, scarf-like, round my neck.

We laugh and joke and remember the play. Vanya is making faces out the window. On Kutuzovsky Prospekt a black BMW with a broken headlamp and tinted windows draws alongside. Vanya sticks out his tongue.

"That's enough. You'll upset them."

A couple of hundred metres on the BMW forces us up on to the pavement.

"We'll soon sort this out!" Sonya composes her features into a naive, seductive expression. Meanwhile, a large man emerges from the BMW of the type who, in the early 1990s, through inertia from their time in the army, had their hair cut short but now wear it long, like an Italian male model. Anyway, this long-haired neanderthal gets out in a crumpled track suit holding an ordinary household axe with a wooden handle. The kind you use for chopping kindling.

Sonya's seductiveness vanishes instantly. She snaps on the central locking.

"Merde!" Masha exclaims. Cars are driving past. The pavement is full of people. The streetlights are bright. This is a street the president drives down twice a day. The man walks straight towards us in a jerky, irregular way. It isn't far, only about five metres. Now he is standing in front of the car. He swings the axe. The girls in the front seat instinctively shield themselves with their arms. I screw up my eyes. The man brings the axe down.

Sonya: "What... what are you doing, you asshole." She is feeling around for any weapon: a bottle of water, a comb... The man tugs the axe out of the punctured bodywork and gives us the scowl of a fearsome avenger, as if we had raped his fifteen-year-old daughter or burned his native village to the ground, and goes back in the same jerky way to his wheels.

Masha: "We can't just... perhaps we should, how do you say in Russian? – point out to him..."

Sonya jumps out.

"Stay here!" I say to Vanya, and open the door. We've really landed in it! Why does he have to pull faces! I'm about to get an axe in my brains and he'll be sent to an orphanage. Or what if I'm just crippled, or mutilated? Get a finger cut off, for example, or an ear? It's a bit late for me to become another Van Gogh.

"Hey, bollock-brain! What are you doing smashing up my car! What have we done to you? The boy stuck his tongue out!" Sonya rages. The man turns round. Sonya jumps back. He still has the axe in his hand. "You stupid bastard! Bollock-brain! Eunuch!" Passers-by turn to look as they hurry along, but do not stop. "You freak! Who's going to pay for the repairs?"

A second man emerges from the BMW, very closely resembling the first. That's it. The end. Curtains. That kind don't forgive. Best if they just kill us now. The second one, however, behaves even more unexpectedly than the first. Instead of rushing at us, he tries to reason with his friend.

"Taras, take it easy, pal! Taras, just forget it, will you!"

The axeman doesn't respond, mumbles something, pushes his friend aside and takes a swing with the axe at Sonya. Luckily his friend grabs it. They stand there in freeze-frame, one with the axe raised above his head, the other holding his arm. They resemble the statue "The Worker and the Collective Farmer", only in this case it's more like two lumberjacks, one trying to relieve the other of the tool of his trade. They stand motionless for what seems like an eternity. Availing herself of the opportunity, Sonya gives her attacker a good kick in the shins. He is about to kick back and then, as if having thought something through, gives up the fight for possession of the axe, swings round and slaps Sonya resoundingly in the face.

"Hey, what are you doing?" I shout, unleashing my inner indecisive intellectual, and clumsily leap on him. I really have no wish at all to come anywhere near this pumped-up muttonhead. It was one thing for me to smack Sonya on the mouth, but it is quite another to defend her from two cavemen. My attack comes to an immediate and inglorious end as I earn myself a punch in the solar plexus. I fall, my head striking the back of the BMW. Unable to breathe, I get a further kick in the ribs. It hurts, the bastard.

I hear shouts, "Dad!"

"Taras, give over!"

"Aaargh, you bitch!" Vanya has got out. I told him to stay in the car. I am trying to breathe, ouch, that's sore. I have wet asphalt in front of my eyes with a layer of gravel. On one of the stones I notice a small spiral. Millions of years ago, a sea shell was fossilized, and now it's landed up here, millions of years later.

I really have no wish to get up. Perhaps I should just lie here in the roadway. I feel the end of the string of sausages under my hand. Did I really jump out of the car with a string of sausages round my neck?

I see Vanya belabouring the guy over the head with a book. No, not a book, a bread board. No, not a bread board, Saint Sergius. Vanya looks truly like a Christian avenger in his watermelon-coloured coat and orange shirt-front, and he is hitting the target. The guy is howling with pain. Vanya has not been entirely sportsmanlike, thumping the guy while he was again being restrained by his friend.

Next to the bus stop, a woman is selling frozen fish. An elderly lady is selecting a carp. At the bus stop, a young mother with a baby in a push-chair and a professor with a neat briefcase are waiting. With considerable conviction, they are pretending nothing is happening. The axeman breaks free from his friend and seizes Vanya by the throat.

"Forgive him! He is shell-shocked!" the friend shouts apologetically, and again tries to restrain his turbulent companion. Masha jumps out of the car, grabs a very long, frozen cod off the vendor's tray and, wielding it like a baseball bat, whacks it with great force into the back of the ruffian's head.

"I've a good mind to call the police!" the vendor mumbles.

Masha strikes again and again until he releases his grip on Vanya. I limp over, clutching my side.

"Don't hit him on the head, he's got concussion!" the friend yells at Masha. Masha hurls herself at the friend. The fish in the hands of Marie Letizia-Geneviève is thawing by the minute and turning into a loofah. Vanya is finishing off the ruffian with the icon.

"Police!" the vendor finally shrieks. "Police!"

I grab Vanya's hand. Enough! Not seeing who it is, he cracks me over the head for good measure. Not with the flat of the icon either, with the corner. He immediately recognizes me and rubs my head to make it better. Sonya runs up, tears off my sausages, and runs back to the ruffian. He is crawling about on all fours, clutching the back of his head. Sonya loops the sausages round his neck and sets about strangling him, the sausages being encased in durable polythene packaging.

"Oh, you bastard! You forty-year-old douchebag! You've divided the whole country up among yourselves! You've grabbed all the best positions and left nothing for us young people!"

A trolleybus trundles up to the stop. The professor helps the young mother get her push-chair and baby up the stairs and into the bus.

"Leave him!" Masha says, picking up the axe from the roadway and dragging her sister off the hapless lumberjack. "Let's get out of here!"

Vanya militantly raises the icon in front of him and makes the sign of the cross over everyone. Sonya breaks free, runs back to her enemy crawling about on the ground, retrieves the squashed sausages, and gives him one last kick.

Back in the car, she doesn't immediately manage the pedals properly. The engine stalls, but finally the Jeep jerks convulsively and we race away.

"Lucky the engine wasn't damaged," I volunteer, trying to accentuate the positive.

"I cut my hands to ribbons on that fish! Frozen fins are sharp! And what a stink! Yuck!" Masha curses, examining her bloodied fingers.

"Masha, you really gave it to them!"

"Second place in the Paris Under-21s Kickboxing Championship."

Part Two

"What a lot of apples!" Sonya exclaimed as we entered the dacha. She took a juicy bite out of the reddest one. A door slammed upstairs. "Who's up there?"

"Only a draught, probably."

"Where is this from?" Sonya asked, pointing to the picture frame propped against the wall.

That damned frame! Vanya and I had forgotten to remove it. Steady. It could have come from any picture frame business.

"It's just a frame."

"I can see it's a frame, but why is it empty?"

"Some friends gave us it, but we haven't yet decided what to put in it."

How about that? I was pleased to find myself such an accomplished liar. The answer seemed to have satisfied Sonya and she switched to domestic topics.

"Where is the kitchen? Let's have a feast. Oh, no! Look at that!" she exclaimed, losing interest in the whereabouts of the kitchen. The object of her admiration turned out to be Grandma's old felt boots, all patched and stained. Sonya hopped around, shoving a leg sheathed in reticulated stockings into one of them.

A window pane rattled. We all looked round. "Only the wind."

I carried the shopping bags into the kitchen and started taking dishes off the sagging shelves of the old sideboard. I saw my reflection in the mirror at the back of it, as if I were at the bottom of a well. My forehead was grazed where the icon had impacted.

The plates were dusty and I needed to rinse them, but no sooner had I turned the stopcock back on when a fat cockroach ran like lightning along the side of the sink. I almost cried out in shock, but it turned out not to be a cockroach. It was a dry parsley leaf, left in the sink from the last time we were here. When the water came on it had been displaced. In any case, we don't have cockroaches in the dacha.

I took the clean plates through to the table. Masha had already put a bunch of tulips in a glass vase with three stripes: yellow, crimson, and black. It looked like a woman in a tight turtleneck sweater. Sonya was cooking something on the stove, filling the kitchen with steam. Vanya, still wearing his watermelon jacket, was running the vacuum cleaner over the floor. Masha had iodine put on her fingers and was now lounging on the couch, chewing an apple, and reading "Chuk and Gek", a children's story published back in time immemorial.

"Do you have a basement?" Sonya asked, not looking up from her cooking.

"Yes."

"I love basements! I bet there are jams and pickles stored down there."

"There should be something."

"And do you have ghosts?"

"Prior to your arrival, we hadn't noticed any."

"Masha, look after the aubergines!" Sonya called. "Come on, show me the basement."

Masha began reluctantly stirring something in the frying pan, while Vanya offered to light the way for us with a torch. The trapdoor in the floor was raised and cold air greeted us. The torch lit up steps.

There were cobwebs in the corners. On the shelves, dusty jars of jam, pickled gherkins, tomatoes in brine, and homemade ratatouille.

"What have we here?" Sonya's eagle eye spotted a couple of cans with no label.

"Old tinned food. A friend of my grandfather's who was a submariner gave him these a hundred years ago."

"Shall we try them?" Sonya gave us a conspiratorial glance, as though we had found an ancient book of spells and were going to cast one just to see what happened.

"Let's do!" Vanya said, and grabbed the cans.

"It might be better to throw them out. We might poison ourselves," I said doubtfully. "They will have gone off. Look at the date on them. 1983!"

"The can hasn't blown, so they're fine."

We grabbed a jar of tomatoes along with the cans.

***

"Aubergines au gratin!" Sonya solemnly announced. "Plus, fried combat sausages with the local spécialité of tomatoes in brine! The sausages are a little battle-scarred." She mimed strangulation. Accompanying Sonya, Vanya made a number of theatrical gestures resembling the obeisances of painted film actors in wigs and powder.

Sonya's bosom was sporting a plastic brooch in the form of two red lips.

"What's that glinting on your tits?" Masha enquired.

"Mumsy's gift! I forgot all about it, but just now found it in my pocket and was sure you would like it!" Sonya tapped the brooch and it played a catchy tune. "Mother's friend gave her it. Two raunchy old women! Do you like it?"

"Very much!" Vanya said, blushing.

"Vanya could do with one of those. He likes hanging about by the roadside. With a brooch like that he won't get run over."

"So what does Vanya do by the roadside?"

Me and my big mouth! I kicked Vanya under the table. "Dad, why are you kicking me?"

"Your dad is embarrassed by what you get up to," Sonya said, pressing a cold tin can to her black eye.

"Er, yes. Vanya wants to bring his collection of treasures to the apartment. We have a disagreement about that. So, what have we here?" I take a great interest in the food on the table.

"I've heated up one of the cans. It's meat with mushrooms."

"How amazing! It's been lying in the cellar for all these years, and here we are eating it."

"We were a great nation, there's no two ways about it. Even the food was canned to last for centuries," Sonya said, sighing nostalgically.

"That's an original idea," Masha laughed, "cooking meat and mushrooms for future ages."

I opened the wine. "Here's to Vanya!"

"Delicious!" The contents of the unlabelled cans exceeded all expectations. Vanya even forgot his vegetarianism. Sonya's aubergines were also entirely palatable. She was a good cook.

Her coat fell off the hook. "The tab has probably torn."

"I'll put it back up." The tab was still intact.

We opened the other tin and Sonya gave everyone second helpings. Taking another forkful, I froze. Among the tomatoes, the mushrooms, the olives, and specks of cheese, in the very spot from which I had just speared a cube of aubergine, a dark hair lay coiled in a pool of the sauce and juice emanating from all the appetizing ingredients. Like a snake, lurking treacherously under a stone.

"How is it?" Sonya asked, pushing back a strand of dark hair on her forehead.

"Oh, very good," I assured her, trying to sound sincere. I surreptitiously manoeuvred the hair to the margins of the plate with my fork. I shut my eyes, thoroughly chewed what was already in my mouth, swallowed it, and drank deeply from my glass of wine.

"We have gateau to come!"

"I'll get it!" Vanya rushed off to get the cake, rattled about in the fridge, and returned bearing a cardboard box. He spent a long time carefully undoing the string.

"Have we got any candles?" Sonya asked.

"I know where there are lots of candles!" Vanya exclaimed, holding up a plump index finger in the manner of a showman. "I'll get them, Sonya!"

After a brief interval of fussing with kitchen drawers, Vanya returned with a bundle of taper-like church candles and a collection of striped milkshake straws, all of which he deposited dramatically in the middle of the table. I was ashamed to see that these were straws filched twenty years ago when the first McDonald's opened in Moscow. They'd been washed many times and had bits of fruit juice stuck to their insides.

"Vanya, why the straws?"

"We can use them with the candles!" Vanya began sticking them into the cake, and then sticking candles into the straws. They were a perfect fit. A forest of faded, striped straws grew on the cake, crowned with Orthodox candles. The forest did look as if it had been hit by a hurricane, with the candles leaning in all directions.

"Where did you get so many church candles from? Are you fundamentalists?" Masha asked.

"We love God!" Vanya said, and crossed himself.

"It's a real designer cake," I enthused. "Just right!"

The candles were lit but, because they were so close

together, withered rapidly, like time-lapse flowers on a television nature program.

"Vanya, blow them out! One, two, three!"

Vanya took a deep breath, becoming almost spherical, and blew with all his might.

Many of the candles bent or fell over and went out, but then, even the ones which had fallen, re-ignited. Vanya blew again. Some went out completely, but the wicks of others flared up. At that, we all started to blow, and the efforts of four pairs of lungs extinguished the recalcitrant flames.

"What kind of candles are these that you can't blow them out?"

"They are probably special candles which can't be blown out by the wind during church processions," Masha surmised.

The candles flared up again.

***

When we had cleared the table, we moved to the couch in front of the stove. Ages ago, I had stripped off the whitewash surround and got a workman to replace the cast-iron door with glass. I love scrubbed brick, and the glass door turned the fire-box into a television. Logs crackle, sheaves of sparks from damp firewood fly upwards like fireflies and disappear into the chimney. Fire grows on the logs and bends like grass in the wind. Tongues of flame flicker to either side, exposing splits in the black wood.

Ribbons of smoke stream like translucent scarves. In the inferno, in the middle of the burning wood, is a formation of orange-white flickering lava. It flutters like an artificial gas fire. The logs split into slices, into honeycombs full of silver ash honey. The fire runs through them gently like Romeo's fingers through Juliet's curls. Sometimes, for no apparent reason, Vanya, with the demeanour of a competent host, stirs up the fire-box with a poker. The logs hiss and crackle.

Sonya is turning the big, ivory knobs on the old Rigonda wireless set. The slider moves over the glass panel, which has cities in every part of the world marked on it. There is hissing and snatches of talking: Russian, German, French. A green light glows in the corner of the display. Finally, there is some quiet music.

"Hey, Vanya. There was one thing I didn't understand in this play. Why, after they've been poisoned, do Romeo and Juliet jump up and start dancing?" Masha asked languidly.

"Juliet poisoned herself and Romeo so as to be born."

"How d'you mean, to be born?" Masha continued, not taking her eyes away from the fire. "They were dead."

"No, by taking the poison, they were born."

"Do you mean, death is being born?"

"No, of course not!" Vanya roared with laughter at Masha's obtuseness. "It's just the poison allows him to be born!"

"But the poison will make him die!"

"Not die but be born!" Vanya enunciated syllable by syllable to make it easier to understand. Everybody sat there thinking, gazing at the fire.

The silence was again broken by Masha. "Let us tell each other stories."

"What about?"

"Oh, I don't know. Something scary."

"Well, okay. You start."

"One summer…"

"A school essay on the topic of 'What I did in the summer holidays'!" Sonya interrupted, laughing. I laughed too, although what was so funny? Vanya laughed too, and so did Masha.

"In short, when I was very little, I lived with my Russian grandmother in the countryside," Masha began.

"That was our shared grandmother," Sonya chipped in. "My father sent me to her for the summer one year, then Masha the next, and sometimes both of us together. That summer, though, my mother took me to the seaside."

"Yes, well anyway grandmother bought me some baby chicks."

"Yellow ones?" Vanya asked, sounding like an expert poultry breeder.

"Well yes, ordinary yellow chicks, two weeks old. Fluffy little snowballs."

"Bundles."

"Well, yes."

"Very scary! A-ah-aaah ...." Sonya did an impression of a wailing ghost. Vanya laughed loudly. Masha asked her sister to stop interrupting, but she too began to laugh, and I joined in. When everybody had calmed down, Masha went on.

"We gave them a place to live in a shed and made them a special little corner. I gave them porridge, and made sure they had water…"

"Water!... Ha-ha-ha!" Through the laughter, it did strike me as strange to be so amused at the fact that long, long ago someone had given yellow chicks water to drink.

"But the next morning we found that one chick had been eaten." Masha was barely able to finish the sentence and everybody roared with laughter.

The first to recover was the storyteller. "What's so funny about that?"

"Who'd eaten it?" I broke in.

"Your grandmother?" Vanya began narrowing down the circle of suspects. It was so funny we had tears in our eyes.

"Not my grandmother, but a hedgehog! We had a family

of hedgehogs living under the house and the mangled chick was on their conscience."

"Hedgehogs with consciences. Imagine!" Sonya said, hiccupping with laughter.

"For six days in a row, we lost a chick every night, but on Saturday night the hedgehogs made a real massacre. They herded the chickens into a gap and ate them alive. The next morning, Grandmother and I found the half-eaten remains of the chicks between the boards and I threw a terrible tantrum. I wanted revenge. I called the hedgehogs fascists. Do you remember that it was the worst thing you could call someone? When I went back to Paris with my mother, everybody at school was amazed that I called bad boys fascists. Grandmother, of course comforted me, but I, – how do you say it in Russian? – was exceptionally brutalized. When my father came, I demanded that he kill the family of hedgehogs. At first, he tried to distract me with a butterfly net, but I was stubborn, capricious. I refused my meals. I so wanted those hedgehogs dead that my temperature even went up. Then my father, looking very sad, put a saucer of milk outside the house and lured all the hedgehogs to it. He put each one in a box. They have such grey, serious little faces. When all the hedgehogs were in the box, my father looked at me one last time but found no clemency. He went to the box, took the biggest hedgehog, threw it on the ground, and stuck it with a fork…"

"A pitchfork!" we all chorused.

"Well, I don't know all these special names," Masha excused herself coquettishly. "So, then, he stuck it with a pitchfork. My grandmother tried to cover my eyes, but I told her not to. I watched, but my father turned away. After the first one was killed, something inside me… how can you say it?…"

"Stirred?"

"Shuddered?"

"Yes, probably shuddered. But I decided to be consistent, like an adult, and not give in to emotions. My mother taught me always to see things through to the end."

"How old were you then?" Sonya cross-examined her.

"Seven. It was my last summer before school." Masha exhaled a cloud of cigarette smoke. "Anyway, father began, not looking, to plunge the fork into the box where they were. I remember the sound. Doob-doob-doob. The hedgehogs did not even squeal. Father hacked at them like crazy, and then I understood."

"What did you understand?"

"Well, everything in general. I never went to my grandmother's again. My father stopped seeing me so often. We never talked about it."

"It wasn't because of that," Sonya said. "He just wasn't capable of living for long in the same family." There was a silence. Logs crackled.

"Don't be upset about it. As a child we have all done a lot of awful things. I even tried to kill Mumsy," Sonya remarked, breaking the silence.

"To kill your mother?" I growled ominously, and everybody burst out laughing all over again.

"Tell us about your mother! Tell us!"

"She was called into my school and given an official reprimand because of me. 'Your daughter is coming to school in worn-out trainers.' Those Soviet freaks! Rather than stand up for her only daughter, my mother came home and whipped me with my own skipping rope. Well, then I really did try to do her in."

"How?"

"I broke thermometers in her room. Mercury is very

dangerous, and I sprinkled it all over my mother's room. I did that for six months. I thought it would kill her, but it didn't. She's alive and well to this day. Ha-ha-ha!"

"Ha-ha-ha-aa-aaaaaa!" Vanya joined in. "I can kill too!"

"Vanya, cool it," I said, touching his shoulder, but for some reason I also found it hilariously funny.

"Who are you going to kill?"

"Look!" Vanya jabbed a finger at the stove.

"Look where?"

"There!"

"Vanya, that's the stove. Are you planning to whack our poor old stove?"

"Not the stove!" Vanya laughed. "There's a hole there. Look!"

There really was a gap between the bricks. At Vanya's insistent request, I moved closer to it. Heat enveloped my face. I could see the orange haze of the fire through the crack. I felt like I was snooping on some unbridled act of passion.

"Very pretty, but so what? What are you intending to kill?"

"Fire!" Vanya pushed in the damper. The tumult in our fiery television stopped, the flames subsided and almost went out, and through cracks in the door and that gap between the bricks, smoke puffed out. It clawed at our eyes and invaded our nostrils.

"Vanya, stop it! We'll suffocate!" I pulled the damper back out and doubled over, pressing my hands to my eyes. "Killing fire: meet the new Anti-Prometheus!"

Everybody burst out laughing again. I rubbed my eyes and chortled.

"Hey, are you all right? Why are you guffawing so much?" Giggling, I looked at Sonya. I thought she seemed incredibly funny. So did Vanya, and Masha, and my own question. "You didn't put something in the aubergines did you?"

"Nope."

"Perhaps someone put the evil eye on the tomatoes? Mum said Timofeyich's wife was envying us our tomatoes," Vanya suggested.

"Your tomatoes? Ho-ho-ho!" Masha suddenly laughed scabrously.

"The cans!" I exclaimed.

"That's it! They were canned food for the armed forces, and old."

"That submarine captain gave them to Grandpa!"

"They mix something in with it, so the men don't freak out in that confined space…"

"You mean, we've just eaten spiked stew?"

"Yep!"

"Ha-ha-haaaaa!" Vanya guffawed, by now quite raucously. Sonya responded, "Tee-hee-hee." Masha was grunting like a pig, and I couldn't keep a straight face.

"It's even had all that time to brew, so to speak! Since 1983!"

"I haven't eaten meat for the last hundred years. You don't think it'll make us ill?" Masha wondered, trying to hold in a gathering fit of laughter.

"It won't make us i-i-ill, yarooo!" Vanya roared, grabbing Sonya's hand. He dragged her off the couch and started dancing with her in a very strange manner. She offered no resistance.

"Vanya, Vanya, wait! Why are you being so wild?" I shouted.

"I'm be-ing wi-i-ild, ha-ha-ha!" Vanya hooted, abandoning Sonya and galloping round the living room on his own. I was doubled up with laughter, but somewhere in the depths of my consciousness I sensed a whiff of danger. He had a weak heart!

"Let's have some tea!"

Vanya was having none of it.

"What are you getting at him for? Are you sad! You'll be taking out a bank loan next! A mortgage!"

"Mort-gage! Ha-ha-ha!" Vanya echoed as he galloped by.

I turned round. Maria-Letizia-Geneviève had already half pulled the cover off the piano. What had suddenly revived her? She'd been slumped just a moment ago like a sack of potatoes, but now her fingers struck the ivories and she burst into song.

Alack, beneath the pine tree, 'neath the tall,

        green pine tree

Take my poor bones and lay me there to-oo-oo rest...

Masha speaks almost without an accent. It appears only when she is nervous or singing. She tends to come unstuck on the vowels. They stagger like a drunk but do not fall. For example, "there" comes out sounding like "thaire". Pausing dramatically, Masha suddenly shrieks, "Eh-eh-eh-ekh!" and plays and sings with as much abandon as if she'd been brought up in a Russian tavern:

Ka-linka, Kalinka, Kalinka, my love!

Little berry in my orchard...

Her fingers, daubed with iodine, run up and down the ivory keys. The singing and the playing come faster and faster. Vanya grabs the cover from the piano, wraps it round himself, shrieks and dances.

I shuffle my feet over to Masha and shout in her ear, "He's got a weak heart!"

She doesn't reply, just gives another shout and waves

me away. I survey our living room: a Down wearing a piano cover as a toga is trampling underfoot our modest apple crop, a speculator in third-rate paintings with a black eye is lifting up her skirt, and the whole disorderly den is under the direction of a French kickboxer who has eaten a surfeit of outdated canned food steeped in uppers. Sonya sticks two fingers in her mouth and whistles piercingly. She casts off the felt boots, peels off her fishnet tights, and begins twirling them over her head.

Oh, my green, my tall green pine tree
Still now your le-e-eaves above my grave!

Vanya pulls a sock off his foot, falls over, and also starts whirling around, imitating Sonya. She puts her tights round Vanya's neck and draws him towards her. He clumsily puts his arms round Sonya. Oh-oh-oh, what's going on?

Kalinka, Kalinka, Kalinka my love!

Pale sprigs of flowers on the grubby, faded pink wallpaper pulsate in time to my heartbeat, moving towards and away from me. There is something dark on the piano keyboard. She's stained it with iodine. It's going to be some job to get that off. I look more closely: it's blood! Masha's cut fingers have started bleeding again! She doesn't notice. She carries on thumping the keys and hollering,

Ekh, Kalinka...

There is more and more blood, wherever Masha's fingers touch the keys. I shout at her but she doesn't hear.

This whole bedlam is brought to its culmination by the person who instigated it: Vanya. Planting a clumsy kiss on Sonya's cheek, he grabs his backpack, unzips it and pulls out – how could I have missed it? – Vanya pulls out of his backpack the painting, folded in four. I didn't know he was carting it around with him.

My dearest son first throws himself down on one knee,

as if presenting the painting to Sonya. She curtsies, not seeing what is in front of her.

"Vanya!" I shout, and make some absurd gesture of interdiction. I go towards them.

He doesn't even turn. He unfolds the painting and begins waving it about like a matador waving his red rag at a bull. Everything flashes in front of my eyes: the naked woman dripping with oil, Sonya with her black eye, the bloodstained hands of Maria-Letizia-Geneviève.

Little berry in my orchard, Kalinka my love!

Vanya flings the canvas to the floor, jumps on a chair, unbuttons his trousers, and begins to piss. The stream is accurately targeted on the body of Petroleum Venus. The music has stopped. All that can be heard is the sound of piss on canvas. The last drops fall in total silence. Incidentally, it isn't by any means every Down who can urinate without assistance.

Behind my back, Masha flicks her lighter. She inhales deeply.

"O, putain! Blood!"

Everybody turns as she screams. Masha stares at her hands and crashes out.

***

She quickly pulls herself together again. I am making a lot of unnecessary fuss. I sit down, stand up, ask Masha how she is feeling. Would she like some water? Oh, there's no need. The silence becomes protracted.

"Vanya, why did you piss on the painting?"

"I love you!" Vanya says, putting his arms round Sonya. "And you." He gives Masha a hug. "And Dad!" He puts his arms round me. "I love you all! I want to dissolve in your world!"

"Does that mean you have to piss?" I'm looking for a rag to dry the painting and the floor but can't find one. Where's it gone? Where's the rag?

"Why are you poking around like that?" It's Sonya.

"I'm looking for a rag." Sonya holds out a pack of tissues.

"How else do you dissolve in the world?" This from Vanya.

Wanting to dissolve in the world is a perfectly reasonable aspiration, and how else would you do it? You can only do it by pissing on this world. I wipe the Venus and the floor. Oh, come on. Why is nobody saying anything?

Sonya seems to hear what I am thinking.

"I see now where the frame came from."

"Vanya, go and wash your hands," I say, tossing crumpled tissues in the fire. He runs away, shouting,

"I'll be right back, Sonya!"

I told them everything. The sisters listened attentively. Vanya corrected me where he thought I was not being accurate enough. For example, he didn't allow me to omit the details about the dying Sazonov.

"I saw the car go bang into the post!" Vanya acted out the accident, putting his drama lessons to good effect. "I looked in and the man was lying there." Vanya demonstrated how Sazonov was slumped against the steering wheel. "And she was right beside him." Vanya stroked the still damp canvas lovingly.

"Why didn't you tell us all this straight away?" Masha finally raised the obvious question.

"We... we... we decided to hold on to it for the time being."

"For as long as your dad was in our grave!" Vanya shouted, laughing. The boy has a practical streak.

Sonya gave a half-smile. "A logical move, except that

the picture is no longer our property. It has been paid for. My father was delivering it to the customer, and I know who that was."

"Of course, we are prepared to give it back," I said not entirely confidently, and with a glance in Vanya's direction.

"She is my mother. I won't give her back!" Vanya stated unequivocally.

"Vanya, don't talk nonsense. What do you mean, she's your mother? It's a woman you don't know, and what's more, it's a painting!"

"I won't give her back!"

"Perhaps we should get some fresh air? You can show us the scene of the crime at the same time," Masha proposed.

***

It was dark outside. In the sky the moon looked like a stale piece of cheese from a leftover sandwich.

"What air! Moist, cold!" Masha spun round, breathing deeply.

I stumbled over something and almost fell. "Damn! What on earth is that lying in the middle of the path?" I saw I'd been tripped by a pitchfork. "Who left the pitchfork there?" I lifted it and leaned it against the house wall.

We went down into the ravine. The beam of the torch picked out a pile of white bags of trash, the cabinets of old radio and television sets, the white carcass of a refrigerator.

"This is dreadful. Why do you treat the countryside so badly here?" Masha gulped.

"When you like something, you say 'we', and when you don't like it you say 'you'," Sonya teased her sister.

I felt bad, as if I'd dumped all this rubbish here myself.

"Is there really no special container provided?" Masha expostulated.

"There is, but most people can't be bothered to drag their rubbish there, so they just dump it here. There used to be ponds here, a series of them. There were water lilies left from the times when there was an aristocratic estate in this place. When I was little we used to sail here on a raft, but when the price of land went up, they drained the ponds to sell plots to developers, only nobody bought them."

"Masha is very concerned about the environment," Sonya said, explaining her sister's mood. "She doesn't even throw out batteries here. Instead she takes them with her back to France, where they have special collection points for recycling them."

"Well, why not? Batteries do terrible harm to nature! You, that is, we, well in short Russia doesn't have special waste disposal sites for batteries. There used to be one place in Moscow I could take them, but then it turned out they were re-packaging them and passing them off as new. You simply don't know how to live in an eco-friendly way!"

"But how do you live in an eco-friendly way?" Vanya asked.

"You don't pollute nature. You don't take more from the Earth than you need to," Masha tried to explain.

"And can you die in an eco-friendly way?" Vanya pursued his enquiry.

"Of course you can. For instance, I want to be buried, not cremated, when I die. If I am just buried, over time I will turn into oil and be useful to people."

"Why will you turn into oil?"

"Oil is just decayed people, animals, and plants which died millions of years ago. Anybody can choose whether or not to become oil."

"I want to become oil!" Vanya declared. "Like in the picture! Dad, bury me the same as Masha, will you?"

"Okay, okay. One day we'll all become oil."

We came out on to the road.

"This is where the car was!" Vanya jumped out and started running along the dividing lane, acting out the accident.

"Get off the road! And stop shouting!"

Masha looked around her at the place where her father had been killed. Sonya lit a cigarette. "What a sky!" Tiny stars twinkled in the darkness overhead.

"That's the Big Dipper," Vanya announced, pointing randomly.

I remembered an astronomy lesson at school. The light of dead stars just keeps on travelling through space. We admire things which long ago ceased to be there. We study things which are not there. We make our vows on something which is not there.

"Okay, you lot. It's a bit cold. Let's go back now," Sonya said, huddling herself up. Climbing up the steep bank of the ravine along the narrow trail between piles of garbage, we noticed a Russian flag flapping in the wind.

"What is that doing there?"

"Our neighbour Timofeyich nailed it to a post."

The tricolor fabric seemed to be splashing like turbulent waves of the sea.

"Oh, look! Look!" Vanya suddenly yelled.

"What is it?"

"Look, here it is!" Vanya rushed forward, squatted down, and grabbed something. "Ouch, it's prickly!" He pulled his hand back. We ran up. In the dim light of the lantern shining beside our neighbour's house, we could see a little ball of prickles. "A hedgehog! A hedgehog!"

Everyone tried to stroke the hedgehog. It snorted. "What's he doing here? It's winter!"

"I heard on the radio that animals are not hibernating because of the warm weather." Masha looked at the hedgehog apprehensively.

"Let's give it some milk to drink!"

"But how are we going to get it home? It's prickly!" We decided someone should stay to guard the hedgehog, while the rest ran to get the milk.

"I'm freezing! I'll go to the house," Sonya said.

"I'll bring the milk!" Vanya volunteered.

"You won't find the right dish. I'll come with you!" I said. Everybody turned to look at Masha.

"Stay and guard him!" Sonya said, slapping her on the shoulder.

"No."

"What do you mean, no?"

"I'm scared. It's half past midnight and dark. I'm scared."

"But it's perfectly safe here. There's nothing to worry about," I began, but then saw real fear in Masha's eyes.

"Well, why don't you stay, if it's all that safe?"

"Me? It's just that Vanya won't find the saucer if I don't help him."

"Look, there's another one!" A pointed grey muzzle pokes out from under the milky-looking refrigerator. The snout twitches, whiskers quiver. The new hedgehog is sniffing the air. "And there's another one!"

A rustling comes from sacks containing tin cans. One more prickly creature emerges briskly, bigger than the last one. Without further debate on the topic of feeding hedgehogs, we beat a quick retreat towards the dacha. Masha even gets there ahead of me. Locking the gate, I peer towards the edge of the ravine. It seems to me that several snouts are staring intently after us.

***

"We got scared of hedgehogs! That submarine food freaks you out no worse than LSD!" We turned on the lights.

"I'll take them some milk anyway," Masha said. "They must be hungry."

I found a suitable saucer, deep and stable. We filled it with milk. Masha went to the door and opened it. A chill wind blew in. She crossed the verandah and turned to look at us.

"Make it quick or the whole house will cool down!"

She went down the steps, put a saucer on the ground right in front of her, and quickly came back in.

We drank our tea with jam and suddenly realized how exhausted we were. To spare the girls household chores, I set about making up a bed for them in my parents' bedroom. Vanya offered to help, and ran back and forth with sheets and pillowcases. Rather than carrying everything at once, he brought each item separately, although maybe that was all to the good. Just bringing the sheets, which hung down to the floor, almost did for him. He kept getting his feet tangled in them and tripped a couple of times. As soon as we'd finished, Masha went to bed. Vanya, abruptly moving from exhilaration to exhaustion, also went to bed forgetting to brush his teeth.

Without a word, Sonya and I find ourselves sitting by the fire. We feel the heat on our faces. Pale orange tongues of fire with slashes of bright blue, like the feathers of tropical birds. Petals of flame, quivering, press their fiery capitals against the sooty ceiling of the fire-box. Embers twinkle within the logs like the lights of great cities seen from the air. Volcanoes erupt on the logs, lakes of lava bubble. And an end can be put to all these worlds by the simple closing of a damper.

"What are you dreaming about?" Sonya asked quietly.

"I... I'm dreaming about being happy, and for Vanya to..."

"For him to get married, have kids, and defend his Ph.D.?"

"No... just for everything to be all right for him."

Sonya decided to throw another log into the stove. She leaned forward and in the slit at the back of her dress her shoulder blades moved like smooth velvet. While she was busy with the latch on the stove door, I ventured to touch her bare skin.

"Oh, what a cold hand!" she squealed, and covered my hand with her own.

My cold hands always get me into trouble with girls. They want hot hands but, as luck will have it, mine are almost always cold. I don't know why. I have to surreptitiously rub and knead my fingers before making a move; sometimes to sit on them, even to warm them under hot water. Sonya looked at me attentively. I brought my lips closer to hers. She looked away, stood up, and walked over to the window.

"I can't see a thing. What is out there?"

"There's an orchard, then a forest..." I came up behind and put my arms round her. "I'm sorry I hit you that time. Something came over me. And I apologize for Vanya. I'll pay for the damage to your car bonnet."

"I accept your apologies, but don't bother about the money," Sonya murmured, closing her eyes and rubbing her cheek against my cheek, my nose and lips.

"And I'd also like to spend the night with you," I whispered in her ear.

Sonya unclasped my arms and lit a cigarette.

"And what would you like?" I asked a little insincerely.

"I'd like always to be rich. I'd like men always to fancy

me, even when I am a hundred years old! I'd like them to fancy me so much that handsome young men come to jerk off on my grave!" Sonya laughed rather too loudly. "What drivel! It's all the fault of that canned food of yours!"

We were silent again. I peeled an orange, gave her half, and threw the peel into the stove. A sharp citrus aroma filled the air for a moment.

"Why are you afraid of being poor?"

"We've never lived lavishly. I've always earned my own living. Do you know how I first made some money?"

"Tell me."

"In the late 1990s, I worked at a warehouse in the rag trade. One day we had a delivery of women's jackets. They were synthetic, with shiny threads and very downy. They electrocuted you with static, but in the light they were iridescent, like motor oil in a puddle. Some Azerbaijanis really liked those jackets. Their women were crazy for them. We sold the whole lot in two days flat. The Azerbaijanis ordered a new consignment and asked us not to sell them to anybody else.

"Another two truckloads arrived. There was no sign of our customers. We waited for a week. No one. Then along came some other Azerbaijanis."

"Also looking for jackets?"

"They just came in. They were ordinary wholesale customers. When they saw the jackets they literally begged us on their knees to sell them. Well, we had promised not to sell them to anyone else. To cut a long story short, these new guys offered us three times the regular price and the director agreed. They took the whole lot wholesale. We'd never seen so much money at one time. Thirty grand in greenbacks!"

"For the jackets?"

"For the jackets, in one hour. A day later, the first lot of

Azerbaijanis turned up. They raised merry hell, said we'd completely wrecked their monopoly, and started shooting the place up. They killed the director and our security guard. I was in the kitchen cooking our lunch. The Azerbaijanis were not very professional, they just lost their cool. They scared themselves silly and then ran away. Didn't even take the safe with them. I helped myself to the money and quietly walked out through the back door."

For some reason, if a woman is stringing you along, she always starts some irrelevant conversation. I sensed Sonya had treated me to this grisly story just to fob me off. I decided to make one last attempt and put my arms round her, this time more insistently. She resisted. I grabbed her hair. I kissed whatever I could as she turned her face away from me. Our shadow was jumping all over the wall, one minute revealing, and the next concealing that faded Renoir reproduction. "Mother's" face disappeared and reappeared, as if winking at me spitefully.

"Leave me alone! I'll scream! Leave me alone!"

"Dad, stop that!" I pushed Sonya away and turned round. At the top of the stairs to the upper floor stood Vanya in shorts and his nighttime T-shirt. His nappy was bulging under the shorts. "Dad, stop being nasty to Sonya!"

Sonya jumped up and ran to the bathroom. Vanya came resolutely down the stairs, righteous indignation written all over his face. In his eyes I was a shameful rapist. I couldn't help smiling. He looked such an improbable upholder of justice.

"Vanya, I wasn't being nasty to Sonya. We were just, just… playing a game."

"What kind of game is that?" Where has he picked up that language? You would think he hadn't been acting Mercutio in a theatre but the teacher in a kindergarten. He pursed his lips in just the way underfucked schoolmarms do when they enter their didactic mode.

"Well, it's a game... sort of like wrestling. We've played that game together, haven't we," I burbled, clownishly grabbing Vanya and pushing him about.

I heard the tap being turned on in the bathroom, but sobbing was still audible above the sound of the water. I playfully rubbed Vanya's ears and propelled him back upstairs. If he heard Sonya crying, heaven only knows what might happen. He is easily distracted. I tickled him, he giggled and squirmed. I put him to bed and sat beside him until he dozed off.

I went back down to the living room. Out of the corner of my eye I noticed a movement. I seemed to hear little claws scrabbling on the floor, but when I turned there was nothing there. A scatter of goose pimples ran down my back and ended up in my stomach. It was laughable that we got so scared by those hedgehogs. Although, after Masha's story... and it is winter... and there were an awful lot of them... But they probably were just hungry. They failed to hibernate and had nothing to eat.

This house, all these things my grandparents, and my mum and dad acquired, surround me. This is their world, and I've brought here these girls I hardly know who are just one problem after another. I've let outsiders into my world. Into our world. The shadows in the corners seem suddenly to thicken. I'm too scared to turn round. What if someone is behind me? A giant hedgehog? The dead surround me, shaking their heads disapprovingly. I no longer hear the sound of running water in the bathroom. The cold creeps out of the cellar and engulfs me, the fire no longer warms.

Mum... Mum, Dad... Grandpa, is that you? Forgive me

that this whole business with the grave has turned out so badly. What can I do? I'm alone now, just me and Vanya and there's no one to help. Grandma, forgive me for letting her put on your felt boots.

I feel a hard wedge in my trouser pocket. When I picked my grandmother's savings up from the floor, I just shoved the banknotes in my pocket. Here they are now. "Gran, I've found your money. Forgive me. I've found your money."

I look about me. The wireless set, the sideboard with the spines of Stalin's collected works, the sofa, the wardrobe. The floorboards creak under my feet. I walk over to the wardrobe and open the door. I go through the old woollen coats, the dresses, Mum's housecoat. There's something in the pocket, cold, rounded, glass – a bottle of castor oil. In one hand I hold old banknotes; in the other, a full bottle of castor oil.

I lean down and put the money away in the back corner of the wardrobe. I put the castor oil next to it. Someone pats the top of my head. It's Grandma's blouse, the dark blue one with white flowers.

I wipe the sweat from my face and light a cigarette. One of Sonya's.

***

The bathroom door opens, Sonya emerges from her refuge and stands behind me. I don't look round. I can feel her indecision. Her hand touches my shoulder. She kisses me. I don't respond. She kisses me again. Her hot-lips brooch flashes.

"Your lips are flashing."

Sonya presses her breasts against me, as she had that first time in the car when we were overtaking the little Lada. We kiss. Hard, gently, passionately. We hug each other, embrace, heavy, fragrant, yielding silk under my fingers.

I wind her long hair round my hand and run my fingers over her face. Invisible down on her cheek gives her a golden halo in the glow of the fire. The hot air around the stove shimmers like a heat haze in the desert.

Her dress is caught up in pleated folds. I pull off her tights. When I was little, we all wore tights, boys and girls. They were woollen and the colour of Roman palazzos: the colour of an old mustard poultice which is falling to pieces, a withered peach, cinnamon, or cappuccino. After sledging your fill till you drop, you'd come home and collapse on the sofa, and Mum and Dad would each take one side of the tights and pull them off you. Those tights, especially when you had got them soaked sledging, had incredible elasticity, stretching for two or three metres, so my parents soon found themselves in the far corner of the room, while the elastic was unyielding in the vicinity of my belly button. The rooms in a Soviet apartment were just not big enough for stripping off a Soviet child's tights.

But now, twenty-five years later, there is no one to strip off my tights. And anyway, I'm grown up and don't wear them any more. And anyway, they don't make them any more. And anyway, they were hideously scratchy. For girls nowadays, though, the world is their oyster. They can choose from an infinity of tights. They buy the ones they think interesting, and can then afford to lie on their backs, lift their legs in the air, and wait for someone to pull their tights off. Each has a different way of waiting: one coyly covers her eyes, another watches brazenly, but all without exception do it sensuously. Every one is anticipating bliss, which in fact for them has already begun, which you can see in their faces. You tug and tug, and tug and tug.

My parents, happily, did not go on to do what I am now doing with Sonya. If they had, I'd have probably grown up as a psycho, and I'm not a psycho. Sonya's body is luxurious, fragrant and snuggly, the colour of crème caramel. The thing between her legs is like the bud of a tulip, ready to open up any moment now.

"Why are you looking so scared?" Sonya asks laughingly.

"Have you got any condoms?"

"No. How about you?"

"No."

The romance evaporates, as if someone has switched on the light.

"Okay, I'll trust you. You're almost celibate." Sonya draws me to her. Celibate! She's decided to feel sorry for me! She trusts me! But ought I to trust her? Still hesitant, I kiss her breasts, her stomach... Oh, what the hell, let's go for it... The hair on the top of her head is parted unevenly, the parting a white zigzag of lightning. I stroke her bum, just as once I gently, delightedly stroked the steering wheel of my first car.

Afterwards, we lie in silence in front of the fire. Sonya chooses an apple, wipes it with her hand, and bites into it. When she has finished, she throws the core into the stove. She sniffs. A pleasant smell of baked apple fills the room.

"Fire brings out the real smell of everything. What else could we throw in? I wonder what sperm would smell like in the fire," Sonya muses.

I say nothing, just look at the tongues of flame. I'm not interested.

Meanwhile, Sonya's usual dynamism returns. She grabs a tissue from the table, wipes off her breasts the white traces looking like icing on her skin, and throws it into the stove.

"Hey, can you smell?" she taunts me. "I've just sent a hundred of your unborn children to hell!"

I don't move. I don't feel sorry for my unborn children,

and in any case there is no smell. In the corner a fly buzzes, awakened by the heat. It is sleepy and just circles around on the floor without flying up. I look at the boards of the ceiling. The knots and the grain form strange, elongated faces with wide-open eyes and mouths. Those two little knots are eyes, and the big one is the mouth. It's the face like in Edvard Munch's painting "The Scream".

"Do you believe in God?"

"I used to, but then it somehow dissolved away. How about you?"

"I don't know. Probably no rather than yes."

Sonya stood up, stretched, and kissed me. "We need that painting back. The customer is a creditor of my father's estate and they're asking me for a refund." On the stairs she stopped. "You weren't too bad."

The embers breathe, growing bright, then dying down. They look like boiled fish with black skin and bright orange flesh. Grandma's felt boots are lying in a heap nearby, abandoned by Sonya.

I take the torch and go outside for a breath of fresh air before turning in for the night. The sky has clouded over, the stars have gone, and there is just inky darkness. The torch lights up the grass in front of the house and the saucer. The milk has been drunk.

The beam runs over the trunks of the trees and higher. Up there, the clouds, pushing and shoving, are scudding by. "Hey, Lord, are you there or not?" I ask quietly. "I know it's an odd question, but give me an answer. If you exist, it's odd that I should doubt it, and if you don't, then absolutely everything is incredibly odd." I mutter all this with my head thrown back. I look about me with the unseeing eyes of a blind man, turned inward.

"Lord, why have you sent all these clouds? Vanya likes sunlight." I run the torch beam over the sky, like a manager inspecting a dark warehouse. If only a rat would scurry away, or a thief. "It's so impolite, Lord! I'm talking to you and you are not answering!"

My mood changes. "Well, fuck you! I don't need you. Why should I waste my time talking to you? What is there to talk about anyway? Where are you? Why do you never answer? Just what I need, a smug, self-satisfied prat like you!" I pick up the pitchfork leaning against the side of the verandah and make a feint.

"Or is this all a dream, a distorting mirror, a mistake, and I've been born into the wrong world, or not been born at all and I'm dead?" Lunge, jump, turn. Lunge, jump. I dance around the empty white saucer. The hedgehogs have drunk up their milk and left us in peace. I am holding a spear which has been used to kill many of their forebears. Above me is a heaven which chooses not to speak. I am in training. At any moment, battle may commence, but I'll be ready.

***

When I go back into the room, I hear Vanya's laboured breathing. "Vanya, are you okay?" No reply. "Vanya!" He groans. His heart! I start looking frantically for the pills. Where are they?! There they are. I take two and raise his head, put the pills in his mouth. "Swallow them, Vanya, swallow them!"

He is trembling, his chest rising and falling rapidly. "Everything is going to be fine," I say, stroking his brow, kissing his cheek.

"It hurts," Vanya complains.

"It'll be all right soon. You just did too much dancing." I curse myself for my negligence, for partying with

Sonya instead of looking after my son. He's been running about so much today. His breathing gradually becomes more regular. "Right, how are you?"

"Why were you kissing Sonya?" Vanya asks sternly, as soon as he is feeling better. "Me? Sonya?"

"I saw you kissing her! I danced with her. I love her!" Vanya again starts breathing irregularly.

"Vanya, she, she loves you too."

"For me she is holy!"

"Well, that's good. That's fine. You don't want to get overexcited."

"It's not good for me to get overexcited."

"That's right, Vanya. That's quite right. It's not good for you to get overexcited." I stroke his brow.

"Good night, Dad."

"Good night, dear Vanya. I hope you dream about something quiet and beautiful."

"I like the flowers and the sun."

"What kind of flowers?"

"I like white peonies. They look like shaggy dogs."

"Then dream of white peonies on a sunny day."

***

In the morning I walk round the yard, put the pitchfork and the stepladder we used for picking apples away in the shed. It is dark in there, with old rakes, scythes, hoes, and spades leaning against the walls. The shelves are full of tins of unusable paint and cartons of rusty nails. I always hope to find treasure here: an old book or an unopened tin of tooth powder from fifty years ago.

I look up at the roof. Grey rafters, uneven planks, old, leaky roofing material. You can see the sky through the holes. The shed is like someone's world, dark, cluttered, the roof its sky and the holes in the roof its stars. I padlock it and walk back to the house.

Under the cherry trees I see the white of eggshells. Mum used to collect them in boxes at our apartment and then spread them under the trees at the dacha. The shells contain calcium and that was her way of fertilizing the soil, but they decompose slowly, reluctantly releasing their precious element. Mum is already gone while the shells seem almost unchanged.

"Look, Dad!" Vanya shouts, pointing down at the ground.

"What?"

"Dandelions!"

I look. Here and there are ripples of crumpled green shoots with emergent buds. The buds have bright yellow wisps, like chicks' feathers, sticking out of them. Dandelions are preparing to flower in December. All around is a carpet of future flowers.

Sonya comes out of the dacha with a cigarette in her mouth.

"Sonya, look. Dandelions!" Vanya runs to her. I give her a smile. She looks away.

"I have to be in town at three. A customer called. Are you coming with me?"

"Of course. You've got our armchair in the back. Vanya, get your things together."

As I am passing Sonya, she stops me with a question. "How about it?"

"What do you mean?"

"Our business problem."

"I can't take the painting away from Vanya. He would be too upset," I say indecisively.

Sonya throws the cigarette butt on the ground. "Fyodor, I'm not leaving it at that."

***

On the way back, near a church, we were overtaken by a police Ford which stopped sideways, blocking the highway. Sonya braked sharply, almost crashing into the side of it. A traffic policeman, as round in his winter clothing as a child dressed up to go out in winter, halted all traffic. A funeral procession, consisting of a nondescript bus with the coffin, a number of cars of Korean manufacture, and a second nondescript bus full of young policemen and policewomen, crossed the solid double line in the road and stopped at the church.

"Off to the next world with blue lights flashing," Sonya remarked, breaking the silence.

With nothing better to do, the rotund policeman came over to us. Sonya slightly lowered her window.

"Be so kind as to show me your ID." Sonya handed over her regisration and licence.

"Ms Sazonova, why are you driving a car with someone else's registration plates?"

"I beg your pardon?"

"In the certificate your car registration is given as 238, but the number plate is 288."

"That's impossible!" Sonya said, getting out of the car. Masha and I looked at each other in bafflement.

Meanwhile, similar-looking men and women in leather jackets were spilling out of the bus and Korean cars. The men had black trouser legs above black shoes with the toes curved up like Persian slippers. The women, all of them, had their heads covered in a cap of permed hair dyed a light colour. The policemen who emerged from the bus unfurled a banner.

"They make terrible flags, from synthetic material. If they cover you with one of those you're going to sweat. A state which economizes on its symbols isn't worth a bag of beans," Masha opined.

Sonya was joking about something with the cop and he was laughing. From their gestures it was clear he was interested in the hole in the bonnet. Sonya was telling him something funny, waving her hands a lot, flashing her eyes at him. The policeman flirtatiously returned her documents and took his leave. Sonya got back into the driver's seat and turned the ignition key.

"Tell me please, who used a marker pen to change the three into an eight?"

I bit my lip. "It was me," Vanya confessed. "The angel told me we needed to change the number so the suicide bombers wouldn't find us."

"Vanya means those two guys yesterday," I said hurriedly.

"Not the men but the suicide bombers they might send to get us!" Vanya corrected me.

There was an awkward silence. I wanted to sink into the ground. By now they seemed to know everything about us, but I still felt terribly ashamed. What sort of nonsense was that? Suicide bombers coming to get us!

"That was totally stupid!" Sonya spat out. "I barely managed to talk my way out of it. I said a child must have played a joke."

***

We drove the rest of the way in silence. Sonya's appointment was at Metro Kuntsevo. "Just don't say a word, either of you," she instructed. "A certain ballerina has a painting to sell. She is well recommended and asking too little. In short, she's a valuable client."

The ballerina was a skinny little thing, with combed

back hair and a pale, nervous face. Masha moved into the back seat with us.

"Who are these people? We agreed to meet alone!" was the ballerina's first comment, with a nod in our direction.

"Relatives. I'm taking them to the hospital. Just ignore them."

Vanya gave her a friendly smile and inclined his head. The ballerina pulled a small painting out of a bag bearing the logo of a smart boutique and Sonya began examining it. It was a landscape, about forty centimetres by twenty. A grey Dutch sky, a field, a windmill in the distance. In the foreground there was a blemish where the paint had been rubbed away, as if someone had used acetone to remove an improper inscription. It was nothing special. Uninteresting, even.

Vanya took the floor, jabbing a finger at the spot before I could stop him. "What do you call that?"

The ballerina did not even turn round.

"Vanya, don't interfere."

"You want a thousand?" Sonya said.

"Yes."

"But that bit hasn't been painted!"

"Vanya, this is none of your business," I said testily in a low voice, giving him a threatening look and squeezing his elbow.

"Yes, I want a thousand. Euros, naturally. This is a genuine…" the ballerina said, picking at the edge of her bag.

"Oh, wow!" Vanya pressed his hands to his mouth and looked around wide-eyed at all present. Not that he is a financial expert, but I keep him informed about the price of things, and he understands that a thousand euros is a thousand bars of Autumn Waltz chocolate.

"Fyodor, do please quiet down there!" Sonya requested

with a politeness so exquisite that it left little doubt her next utterance would be shrieked.

"You were recommended to me as a high class professional and you turn up to a meeting with morons!" the ballerina squealed, and began clambering out of the car.

"I'm not a moron, I'm a Down," Vanya corrected her.

"Will you just shut up?" Sonya's eyes flashed and she tried to mollify the ballerina. "Wait, please don't be angry. Let's go to a cafe where we can sit and talk in peace."

The ballerina, however, had already jumped out, huffing and puffing and, looking a complete mess, her coat unbuttoned, began furiously thumbing for a lift.

"She'll catch cold like that," Vanya said, looking at me anxiously. "Dad, tell her to do up her buttons. She won't do it if I tell her."

"Vanya, just shut up."

How long we sat there in painful silence, I don't know. The ballerina soon got a lift and departed. Without a word, Sonya moved off.

"Sonya, you, er…" I began.

"I asked you just to sit there and keep quiet," she hissed. "Quiet! For Christ's sake, was that not clear?" She was shrieking now.

"I'm sorry. You…"

"I'm a Down!" she mimicked Vanya. "You've really got something to be proud of there!"

"Sonya…"

"Sonya what? That was an excellent offer. After restoration, I would have flogged that thing for thirty grand. Now I've got sweet FA, and to add insult to injury word will go round that I turn up to meetings with a bunch of retards who join in the negotiating!"

"Easy, Sonya!"

"What do you mean, 'Easy'? You pretend you're as pure as the driven snow but you're just thieves! We'll have you! Won't we, Masha? Turn you over to the cops! And point the owner in your direction!"

"Well, you go right ahead! Grass us up to the cops. We'll just chuck that crappy daubing out, burn it, cut it into tiny pieces and you won't be able to prove a thing!"

"Give us the painting back!"

"Give us our grave back first!"

"Learn to screw properly! And now just fuck off out of my car!"

"What?" I feel myself going red in the face but can't do anything about it. What's she talking about? She looked like... It seemed like… Everything is boiling inside me. I open the door, jump out, and practically end up under a bus. I haul out Vanya, who is thoroughly frightened, and run to the back of the car. I heave at the door and it finally opens. I pull out the armchair in frenzy and slam down the lid. The Jeep noses jerkily into the flow of traffic.

"What about my flowers?" Vanya reminds me.

"Stop!" I yell after them, catching up and hammering on the bodywork.

"The flowers!" Sonya slams on the brakes. I get into the back and grab the bouquet. Masha is good enough to give us a wave. We stand there on the pavement with our armchair and yesterday's bunch of purple tulips.

***

"I love Sonya, and Masha," Vanya says when I've put him to bed.

"Sonya wants to squeal on us to the police and you still love her?"

"I still do. And Masha too."

"How can you love two women at the same time, Vanya?"

"I can. I love them. I've decided to be faithful to both of them."

"Don't you love her any more?" I nod in the direction of the painting. The Petroleum Venus is still in our possession. She has dried out after Vanya's escapade and now hangs on the wall opposite the bed. "You used to love only her."

"I love her too."

"Are you saying you're in love with all three of them?"

"Yes," Vanya says timidly and hides under the blanket.

"And are you going to be faithful to all of them?" I ask, tickling him.

"Yes-ah-ah-ah!" Vanya giggles, squirming.

"Good night, my son." I kiss him on the cheek and turn off the light.

"Good night, Dad. What does 'screw' mean?"

***

I was sitting watching television and trying to figure out what to do if Sonya really did hand us over to the police. Her last retort, adding insult to injury, gave me no rest. "She just said it from spite. She's a spiteful woman," I consoled myself, but couldn't allay the doubts she had sown about my sexual prowess. They spread through my neurons like fire in a hayloft. On top of everything else, our estate agent sent a text refusing to work for us any longer. We were problem clients. Then Masha called.

"Hi! Is it too late to phone?"

"No, has something happened?"

"Something really bad has happened!" Masha was almost crying.

"What is it?"

"Churchill is dying!"

"I thought he was long ago in his grave."

"It's not a joke. He's my cat."

"Sorry, Masha. Don't upset yourself! I can help you find a vet." For some reason, it seemed to me that, as Masha is half-foreign, she wouldn't be able to find a phone number herself.

"I've found one already. I'm at the animal hospital. I know he's only a cat but… I don't have anyone else... you see... no one." Masha burst into tears.

"Oh, dear. There, there, don't cry. What can I do to help?"

"Can you come over? I feel so bad."

"I have Vanya here."

"Oh, yes, of course, sorry. Oh, God, what is happening to me! I'm so tired of this life."

I thought for a moment. "Well, actually he's asleep, so perhaps I could pop round. I'll just take a look."

Vanya is quietly snoring in bed. I get dressed and hurry round to the address Masha gave. It's not far. A twenty-four hour veterinary clinic on the Garden Ring. In the bright fluorescent light of the reception area, everything seems lifeless. Masha is sitting on a bench, leafing through a magazine.

"Hi!"

"How wonderful of you to come!" Masha throws her arms round my neck.

No one could say she let her suffering show. They make them tough in Europe.

"How is he?" I make it my first priority to enquire after the health of Churchill.

"Oh, it's all fine. He is out of danger. I'm so glad to see you! Sonya talked so much nonsense today. She's like that sometimes. I am sorry, okay?"

"Oh, that's all right. It was our own fault. We fouled up

her deal... What was wrong with the cat?" I want to put an end to her apologies and find out exactly why, for the first time ever, I've had to leave Vanya alone and run here in the middle of the night.

"He's been neutered. I didn't think he would survive. He is very young and just started everywhere, how do you say in Russian..."

"Marking his territory."

"Yes, that's it! Marking. It smells so bad, it's horrid! And two weeks ago he fell off the balcony when he saw a she-cat. It's just as well my apartment is on the second floor. He wasn't hurt. I love him so very, very much. He's a pedigree cat, hypoallergenic. Poor thing! Where did you get this?" Masha touched a bone bracelet I wear on my wrist.

"In Berlin... So you decided to have him neutered at night?"

"Well, yes. My whole apartment smells really bad." Masha sits for a moment, thinking. "While I was out here I saw one little dog being taken away in a black plastic sack and, and..." Masha starts sniveling. "And I thought they might put my Churchill in a sack like that..."

Masha puts her head on my shoulder. I stroke it, becoming increasingly incensed. The bitch knows perfectly well that I don't leave Vanya alone, and in spite of that calls me out here for no good reason. She just took it into her mind to chop her cat's balls off in the middle of the night. What touching concern.

"Masha, you'll have to excuse me, I have to go now."

She seems not to hear. "Do you know why my lips are asymmetrical?"

"No."

"When I was a child, I let a powerful punch through while I was training. I've still got the scar."

"Masha, I really must…"

"I understand. It's because of Sonya. She's like that. At first she's très gentille, but then she covers you in shit. It's always the same when she likes a man. She won't report you to the police, don't worry."

"Okay, Masha. We'll sort it out…"

"Vanya's asleep anyway…" Masha brought her face, bluish in the clinical light, closer to mine. That fleck in her eye melted like brown sugar in blue liqueur and made the whole eye dark. My own eyes were jumping like sparrows in a cage.

"If he does wake up and I'm not there... I've got to go."

She suddenly kissed me.

"Masha, I'm sorry." I got up and almost ran out of the clinic.

"Idiot! Your whole life will be like this, nursemaiding your halfwit! Nursemaid! Sonya doesn't need you! Fuck and forget!" Masha shrieked after me.

The metro was already closed. I set off on foot through the empty streets. The streetlights were reflected in the wet asphalt. A path of moondust formed under each of them. In the brightly lit windows of a late-night electronics store, two assistants in white shirts were knocking ten bells out of each other. One punched the other in the teeth and he crashed into the glass door, his split lip trailing a wet red smear over the words "round-the-clock". In an archway near a bar teenage girls were putting on make-up in order to look older. Vanya will be sleeping soundly tonight anyway, because I gave him a sedative...

***

"This is a private party." The security guard rules out further progress verbally and physically. Behind him, the insides of the bar are a-buzz with music and voices. The bar looks like a blobfish, with its mouth gaping as it waits for more small fish to swim in before the mouth slams shut. I turn to leave and bump into a girl with long, luxuriant hair. "Sorry."

"Fyodor?"

For many years I have been imagining this meeting.

For example, in Venice. I would be standing on the balcony of an elegant palazzo, sipping a glass of wine and indolently responding to the caresses of an Italian girl with dark, curly hair and an aristocratic pedigree. Meanwhile, she would be down below among the heaving, ordinary, tourist crowd. She is gawping at everything, taking ridiculous photographs. She has slaved for years to save up enough to go on an "Italy in a Week" tour. She sees me, but I pretend not to know her and passionately kiss my hot girlfriend.

Or we are in St Moritz. I am at the wheel of a 1950s sports car, my only company the skis, a large wad of cash, and the daughter of a Chicago capitalist. She has a haughty, Anglo-Saxon look and long red nails. We stop at the piste, put on our skis and, amazing everyone with our skill, descend at high speed. She is fussing about there, slithering clumsily and falling over next to her flabby husband, who has brought her here on a day trip.

"Hello." Lena is surprised. She takes stock. So many years have passed. Am I looking better or worse? Am I a success or a failure? I really don't know what my face is registering. I don't think I manage to look suave and imperturbable, but the result of that initial inspection seems to be on the whole positive. Although something resembling a maternal look appears in her eyes. I hate maternal looks in women's eyes.

"How are you doing?" I ask. What else do you ask after fifteen years of separation? "Splendidly!" An appropriate response.

A tanned man approaches and gives her a hug. "Fyodor, this is Sergey. Sergey, this is Fyodor."

"Good to meet you!" A firm handshake.

On his chest, under a short, unbuttoned jacket, I read "Mirabel 2007. I was there". I take this to be an allusion to the arrest of a Russian oligarch at the Mirabel ski resort.

"This one's with us," Lena nods at me and we go inside to a fug of music, smoke, and body heat.

"Come to our premiere!" Lena smiles, pulling from her purse two squares of thick glossy paper. "We've filmed a musical. I'm in the lead role. Take them. Each is for two people."

"Thank you." I take the invitations, finger them, and my heart sinks to my boots. The illustration on the invitations is the Petroleum Venus, only without the barbed wire halo and with the added caption, "'Our Alyonushka' from 1 January in all cinemas".

"What is… this?"

"It's a musical, and I'm in the lead role! Why, doesn't it look like me?" Lena laughs loudly and snuggles up to Sergey.

"What do you mean, not like you?" By now I am completely at sea.

"I mean, that's me! In the picture!" Lena turns her face upwards, mimicking the pose of the Petroleum Venus. "What do you think? There's been a real detective story with this picture. The artist died in a car crash and it disappeared. Can you imagine?"

"I certainly can."

"It's a shame. I really liked the painting."

"Perhaps it will just turn up."

"Some hope!" A party of their friends draws them away. "Well, so long! Come over some time. Let's talk!"

Sergey hands his jacket to one of the staff. The back of his T-shirt continues the theme begun on his chest. It reads, "We'll be back", and underneath is a helicopter painted in the style of Khokhloma Russian folk art, firing missiles at a mountain village somewhere in Europe. The age-old chalets are about to go up in napalm flames.

Lena is a beauty! Lena is a film star! Lena has a life of her own! Was there really a time when we were in love? Meetings in the metro, kisses in apartment block entrances. It all comes back to me. I push my way through to the bar. "Vodka, fifty grams!"

I repeat the order. I repeat it again. What on earth is love? Lena's parents believed that love for people like Vanya means saving them from suffering. They are ill all the time, live inadequate lives, suffer ridicule and bullying. To let them live is cruel; taking their life away from them is an act of love. But what about Churchill? Masha snipped off his apparatus not only because of her love of hygiene, but also so that he wouldn't fall from the balcony. Is that not also a manifestation of love, of sorts?

Or is it just selfishness? By castrating her tomcat, Masha provides herself with an amenable toy, a hypoallergenic pet she can stroke without fear of getting herself covered in scabs and swelling up like a balloon. I remembered how my mother, before Vanya was born, always demanded that I should be home no later than ten, so she could keep an eye on me. I so wanted to hang out with my friends in the courtyards, drinking wine in the archways of buildings, but my mother was anxious. "You'll worry me to death with your wild ways!" she cried. Was that love too? If so, it was a pretty mean variety.

On a screen hanging near the ceiling in the corner of the bar an advertisement comes on. "Upload cool pix to your mobile", with a menu of options. A handsome famous footballer, a young mulatto singer, the bare-chested president of Russia, and Jesus Christ. Is that where you've got to, Lord? Inside a TV set? The head of Christ is thrown back, his eyes turned heavenwards. His forehead bears scratches from a crown of what looks like barbed wire. You can't tell from the way he's depicted whether he is suffering or writhing in delicious languor. Under each picture is an inscription appropriate to the character. The caption under Christ reads, "God loves you."

***

Back home, I found Vanya in tears. Our belongings were scattered everywhere. Vanya's rug with its hiding pockets had been torn from the wall, the pockets turned inside out.

"Sonya hit me. She said, 'Give me the picture'."

I clenched and unclenched my fists in fury as I took in the extent of the sisters' perfidy. One had lured me out of the house, while the other ransacked the place! But Churchill was for real. They hadn't castrated him just for plausibility. It was a coincidence. That couldn't have been part of an evil plan. Sonya thought I was home too.

While I was agonizing over these possibilities, Vanya was transformed.

"But I didn't show her where the picture is. I hid it really well!"

***

The next day, the whole gigantic exterior of our apartment block, which overlooks the embankment, was covered by an advertising banner. The excuse was that the block was undergoing repairs. The exterior walls were being painted and so, in order to hide the "unsightly" scaffolding, they had covered everything up with this banner. Representatives of the advertising agency phoned every apartment, inviting us to sign a statement that we had no objection, in return for a bag of New Year's goodies. Vanya sternly demanded to see what was in the bag, and when that turned out to be a bottle of vodka named in honour of the president, a box of marshmallows, and a jar of instant coffee, he forbade me to sign.

"This is a scam! We'll complain to Mayor Luzhkov!" With these words, he took the bag from the agency's activists and slammed the door.

The banner depicted the Petroleum Venus, only enlarged to the size of an apartment block. I felt I'd been caught red-handed. It was as if someone was shouting, "Look, here they are! The thieves are hiding in the apartment just behind her belly button." There was only one drawback to all this. The lady Vanya so adored greatly restricted the access of the precious light he so loved. The residents started collecting signatures for a collective complaint.

"Beautiful," Vanya opined, taking a bite of his promotional marshmallow as we stood in front of the block, admiring the advertisement.

"We've been invited to the premiere," I said pensively.

"We should definitely go!"

"We've been invited by the woman who really owns the painting."

"Sonya?"

"No. Sonya wants to give the painting back to this woman. I think... I think we need to give the painting back to her ourselves. Without Sonya."

"Never!"

"Think about it: she loves her too. By the way, we've got a spare invitation. Who should we invite?"

"We should invite Sonya, and Masha."

"But she hit you!"

"I still love her." Vanya arched himself flirtatiously and began running round in circles, his arms extended like the wings of an aircraft.

All day long I vacillated over whether to invite the sisters or not. And if I was going to invite them, which one should I call? If it had been up to me, I wouldn't have phoned either of them, but that was what Vanya wanted. In the end, I decided to call Sonya. She answered as if nothing at all had happened.

"Have you seen the advertisement?"

"Yes. We're invited to the premiere."

"Good for you."

"You can come with us if you like. It's the day after tomorrow."

"I'll need to ask Masha. Oops, I have a call waiting. I'll ring you back."

Half an hour later it was Masha, not Sonya, who called, and seemed even less discomfited than her sister, as if last night's episode at the vet's had never occurred. "The hairdresser can make two tomorrow at my place. Is that convenient?"

"What hairdresser?"

"To give Vanya a haircut. We are going to a premiere, aren't we?"

"Why does he need a haircut?"

"To look his best. It's on me."

I made a note of the address and looked into Vanya's room. "We'll go to Masha's tomorrow to get a haircut."

"Why do we need a haircut?"

"You need to look your best for the premiere."

"Are you getting a haircut too?"

"We'll see. I might just sit, or go out for a walk while you're having yours."

"I don't want you to leave me alone, Dad!"

"Vanya, you love Masha. What's the problem? In a few days you're going to be sixteen!"

"Don't leave me alone!"

"You need to learn to be independent, to get along with other people. I can't always be there holding your hand!"

"Dad, I don't want to get along with other people!" Vanya burst into tears and ran over to hug me. I pushed him away.

"That's enough sniveling, Vanya! Why do you keep crying all the time, like a girl! You're a grown man already. You asked me to invite Sonya and Masha! She hit you, but you say you love her!"

"Dad, I love you!" Vanya shifts uncomfortably from one foot to the other, trying to take my hands.

"You're all love, Vanya! Just get away from me!" I suddenly yell in an unnatural voice. "I've got you round my neck and you won't let go! Do you enjoy tormenting me? Do you like watching my life ebbing away within these four walls? Is that it?"

I grab Vanya by the shirt and start shaking him. "When did anyone ever want to be friends with you? Two real, normal girls! But no, you have to get in on the conversation, you're the big art expert. 'That bit hasn't been painted!' Who asked your opinion? Now you don't want to get a haircut! Take a look at yourself in the mirror. You look a complete schmuck! The ballerina was right. It's an embarrassment sitting next to you!"

I tug at his shirt tucked into his tracksuit bottoms. "What is this? Don't you even know not to wear a shirt designed to go with a jacket along with tracksuit pants? You've even tucked it into them! No normal person would ever think of doing that! God Almighty, what have I done to deserve this?"

By now I'm not really yelling at Vanya. God knows who I am yelling at. I'm rampaging round the room shouting my head off. "Sonya had every right to hit you! You steal something and don't want to give it back. Who ever heard of such a thing? You rob a dying man! You're a complete monster! I'm not even going to ask you. You'll hand it over and like it."

Vanya is wailing.

"Stop that racket!" I shake him by the shoulders. "Stop howling! Why do you never stop bawling? Talk quietly! Speak to me in a whisper! I hate your yelling!" I take a swing at him. Vanya cowers, waiting for the blow. At the last moment, I lower my fist.

Vanya is quiet, only sobbing occasionally. I'm the one yelling, telling him to be quiet. What have I just been doing? What was all that about? My rage subsides as rapidly as it appeared. I see Vanya's room with all his little things in it. I see Vanya, wiping away his tears and trying to clean himself up. I see myself, the embodiment of malice. I am ashamed, both of the scene I have just created and of the fact that I am ashamed about it.

***

On the pavements there was a pleasant atmosphere of spring-like anticipation of the New Year holiday. Everywhere there were decorated fir trees, like girls in sumptuous, multi-tiered skirts. The shop windows were full of festive bits and pieces.

We descended deep underground to metro stations lined with Stalin's mosaics. From their vaulted walls and ceilings, sturdy collective farm girls bearing sheaves of wheat gazed out; burly boys with frank, simple faces, clutching books;

broad-shouldered soldiers in dress tunics, arm in arm with girl students.

We got on the train and leaned against doors which we knew wouldn't be opening. On the opposite wall, next to a map of the metro, was an advertisement for "Our Alyonushka". Next to the poster, a grey-haired pensioner with pinched features was shifting uneasily. He looked around at his fellow passengers with the eyes of a fanatic seeking moral support. Finding none, he decided to take matters into his own hands. With the key, which all this time had been clenched in his fist, he started scraping at the poster. At first timidly, with furtive glances, but then in a growing frenzy. The pensioner started, needless to say, with the delta between her legs. I could just imagine how wet that key must be with his sweat. A few passengers glanced indifferently in his direction before returning their heads to their previous position: some were engrossed in a crime thriller, but most stared blankly into the emptiness in front of them. I watched the actions of this grey-haired champion of public morality with some curiosity. He psyched himself up by growling words like "whorish", "disgusting" and "...brought the country to..." Carried away by the spectacle, I briefly let Vanya out of my sight, remembering him again only when he himself entered the frame, standing immediately behind the manic scraper. Before I could stop him, Vanya loudly ordered, "Stop that vandalism!"

He said it so convincingly that the pensioner jumped and turned around. When he saw Vanya in front of him, his face stern but evidencing intellectual incapacity, the pensioner became emboldened and retorted, "Keep out of this, lad. Those oligarchs have filled your head full of nonsense!" He'd evidently decided that Vanya's mental problems were the result of the machinations of evil billionaires.

"I have a good head on my shoulders. Victor Timofeyich told me so!"

"Bah!" The pensioner turned and went back to his scraping with redoubled vigour. "It's not polite to turn your back when someone is talking to you!" Vanya persisted. Our fellow passengers began taking an interest. At the far end of the carriage a man with a skimpy moustache stood on tiptoe. The readers of crime novels closed their books, keeping their place with a finger between the pages.

"Cool it, Vanya," I whispered in my son's ear.

"Keep your handicapped friend under control," the pensioner said loudly and rather vehemently, evidently feeling he was being persecuted for his beliefs. He had few teeth left in his mouth and they looked like yellow levers. If you were to pull one, he might produce a shovel and start digging; pull another and a pneumatic drill would come out and start breaking up the roadway.

"No need to be offensive, old fellow." When people refer sneeringly to Vanya's health, it takes only half a pull on the starter handle to get my motor going.

"Leave huh walone. She's pwetty!" Vanya fretted. Lena-Venus-Alyonushka had already had mortal wounds inflicted on her. They cut like white furrows through her beautiful, solarium-tanned body.

"Oh, you stupid ninny! You're all ganging up on me!" The senior citizen went berserk, shaking with indignation like a jelly. In one of his wildly rolling pupils a cataract was making headway. Vanya grabbed the pensioner's arm. The man tried to shake him off. I grabbed the fist with the key. A boy wearing headphones smirked and moved away. The man with the moustache was practically falling over himself, trying to see what was going on. Someone pressed the emergency button.

At the next station, the crowd carried us out of the carriage and straight into the arms of two waiting policemen.

"What's going on here, then?"

"Arrest that vandal!" Vanya squealed and poked the pensioner.

What happened after that made no sense at all. The police set about separating us from the pensioner. Everybody was panting and growling and puffed up with indignation, offended and angry. Nobody uttered a word.

We were all dragged off into the stagnant, subterranean atmosphere of the station's police office, the pensioner in one room, Vanya and I in another.

"Guys, it was nothing, everyone just got a bit overexcited," I said with an apologetic, ingratiating smile. The uniformed gentleman writing the report did not look up. "We just…"

"Name?" the policeman asked Vanya, ignoring me.

"Ivan… Fyodorovich Soloviov," Vanya articulated carefully.

"And how does this man relate to you?"

"He's my dad."

"Then why does your dad not have the same name as you and there's no mention of you, Ivan Fyodorovich, in his passport?"

Vanya tensed, and looked at me anxiously.

"Listen, it's a long story."

"I'm not talking to you, pal. Ivan Fyodorovich, you will have to see a special doctor. You need to be looked after…"

I took out my last five hundred ruble note and laid it on the table. Two hundred would have been enough, but I only had a five-hundred note and didn't feel I could ask for change.

"Our state spends money on you, teaches you in schools,

and look how you behave!" The policeman gave us a good telling off while pocketing the banknote. In parting, he shook hands warmly with both of us.

"What a nice, cultured man," Vanya said after carefully thinking everything over. We got out at Mayakovsky station.

"Look, Vanya, why did you have to mix with that old man?"

"He was destroying beauty."

"It was just a poster. There are thousands of them. There, for example!" I pointed to Venus-Alyonushka pasted on the side of a trolleybus.

"They might have sent you to the loony bin! Have you any idea what that would be like?"

"I love beauty, but he was afraid of beauty. It humiliates him. He calls beauty sinful."

"That's all well and good, but you need to be careful, Vanya. Otherwise you won't survive. We have to pretend we don't notice all sorts of nasty things."

"For me, beauty is the most important thing in the world. For the sake of beauty, I will suffer anything... even the loony bin, even... I am prepared to... to lose my voice," Vanya said suddenly. "And my silence will deafen the world."

**

It turned out that Masha lived in a house on which I had done my first-year fieldwork survey when it was being built. Since then, little had changed. A thick cable ran from a trailer chugging away in the alley. When the house was built, it turned out the electricity supply was inadequate. They scraped together enough for the lights and lifts, but not for air conditioners and washing machines. There was an energy shortage, and the city authorities had not allocated enough capacity. By the standards of the times, the apartments were very smart and had already sold out, so the contractor just brought along a powerful diesel generator, which ever since had been making up the deficit.

The hairdresser, stylist, and manicurist was a wiry little man with a flat, broken nose which made him look like a criminal. If I'd encountered him on the street at night, I'd have crossed the road. Masha reassured us, "Eddie's miraculous, even if he does look like a villain! Go for a walk. When Vanya's had his haircut, we'll all go shopping." Masha blew on her splayed fingers. She had just had a manicure and wasn't allowed to touch anything while the nail varnish dried.

"Shopping? What for?"

"I want to buy Vanya something! Don't argue! How do I look? You haven't said a thing."

Masha had had her hair curled. Her straight white locks now spiraled.

"It suits you very well. You look more, well, sultry now. Although I liked the way you were before." You never know with women whether to compliment them on changes to their appearance or not. If you do, they may decide you thought they looked hideous before. If you don't, they may get upset and think it's been a change for the worse.

"Sultry... Is that good?" Masha asked, coming over to me.

"It's fine. But why do you want to go shopping?" I asked, resuming our conversation where it broke off.

"I want to buy Vanya a Christmas present. Christmas is the day after tomorrow!"

"The Catholic Christmas. Ours is another two weeks yet."

"I don't believe you are a real Russian! The Catholic

one! What difference does it make? Who cares if it's the Muslim one. What matters is the presents! Anyway, you go for a walk. We'll sort all that out for ourselves. Right Vanya?"

A heavily bandaged cat with short grey fur came into the room, evidently Churchill. He didn't look happy.

"Can I stroke him?" Vanya asked, immediately cheering up.

"Yes, but be careful."

Vanya gently reached out and ran his hand over the cat's glossy head.

"What's happened to him?"

"He had a slight accident, but he'll soon be better."

"Off you go, Dad."

"Are you trying to get rid of me? I'll just sit here."

"No, go. You wanted a walk."

"If you like, I can stay."

"No, Dad. That's okay."

***

I wander aimlessly through the streets, feeling as if I've just been released from prison. I even give my hands a shake to make sure I'm not in handcuffs. I twist my neck. No leash. A girl going by gives me a smile. I give her a jaunty wink and am surprised at myself.

The place is buzzing all around me. Top managers, disseminating for a mile around the narcotic fragrance of their high "above-board" salaries, are going for lunch. They come out of their offices in jackets, leaving their overcoats behind. The wind blows their hundred-euro ties over their shoulders and the top managers put them back in place without looking even slightly undignified. Lower-ranking policemen crack sunflower seeds. They all have pudding-basin haircuts with a shock of gelled hair sticking

out from under the cap. They check the ID of stubbly guest
workers with weather-beaten faces. A grey bus is parked
in the square, its windows theatrically curtained with dark
red velvet. The curtains twitch as if waiting for the show
to begin. It will, just as soon as even one daring schoolgirl
turns up with an anti-government slogan. Grey-flecked
special unit policemen will spill out of the bus, their boots
clattering. They will take away the schoolgirl's placard
and drag her by the hair to a van with a barred window.
Two senior schoolgirls, wearing heavy makeup which
disguises the freshness of their complexions, come out of
an Italian lingerie boutique. A Buryat nanny with slanting
eyes and a swarthy face is taking home a pale girl with a
large satchel. Judging by her pallor and spectacles, the girl
is the offspring of an intellectual Moscow family. A young
man with his scarf knotted in Parisian style tries clumsily to
drive a brand new Japanese runabout up on to the kerb. A
parking attendant with a peasant face, gesticulating wildly,
shouts to him, "Turn the other way! Now straight to me."
A homeless boy has curled up in a concrete bowl full of
purple pansies. He's asleep or has crashed out. Some joker
has placed a flower behind his ear. A dachshund, sticking
out a tail as long and pointed as Pinocchio's nose, makes a
puddle at the corner of the flowerbed. The stream flows over
the pavement. I step over it.

I pass numerous cafes. People are sitting inside, eating,
drinking, laughing. My eyes alight on a suntanned female
waist in hipster slacks. The waist develops into a pleasing
bum, flattened by the seat of a chair with its wicker back to
the window. Her dark skin is transected by the strap of her
G-string. The strap follows the shape of her body, slightly
constraining its mistress's rather generous hips. It follows
the dimples on her sacrum, bifurcates, and disappears into

the hollow between her buns. How am I going to live when low-slung jeans for women go out of fashion?

I stroll inside, sit down at a table, look around at the other customers. I casually cast a glance in the direction of the girl with the waist. She has a round face, slanting blue eyes, ears set too low, a flattened nose. Why?! What a sad joke. It's as if I've again found a very long hair in an otherwise appetizing salad. Some evil clown seems to be playing tricks on me. From the back, though... and she has quite a waist. Next to her is a respectable lady, tastefully dressed, with a quality hair-do, well manicured. The mother, even if her daughter is mentally backward, is making the most of herself.

Outside the window, a column of tow trucks appears. Some of the cafe's clients run out to their Volkswagens, Mercedes, and Peugeots, including the mother of the girl with the waist. Her daughter moans piteously, and the mother takes her with her. Through the window I see someone manage to reverse in time and make their escape. The rest go to negotiate with the traffic cop. Scratching his head under his cap, he listens to the hapless drivers' excuses before sending them one by one to his partner in the police car. There the matter will be resolved.

So life goes on. People know a tsunami will come, but still build their huts by the ocean. They park their car in a place from which, sooner or later, it will be towed away. They will have to scour the car pounds located in the outskirts, stand in line, write out a statement, pay a fine, but time after time people do it again. They pay bribes to the traffic cops, get behind the wheel, drive in a circle until the tow trucks move on, and then come back to their original parking place.

While the mother is reaching an accommodation with

the policeman, the Down girl shifts from one foot to the other outside the cafe's enormous window. She is wearing a dark-coloured raincoat in which I suddenly see my own reflection. That is, my face is reflected in the glass while she is outside, and it looks as if I am being reflected in her raincoat. My face appears to be under water. The raincoat's folds are waves rolling over me. The girl takes a step to one side and I disappear.

"Have you chosen?" I hear the waiter ask.

"What? Oh... what do you have? Right." I leaf through the menu. I'll have green tea and a starfruit pastry. Oh, damn! I've got hardly any money. I gave it all to that cop! "Sorry, I have to go."

I wander the side streets again. My mobile rings, Masha's number appearing on the screen.

"Hello. How's it going?"

"Vanya has disappeared."

***

As if in a trance, I run. Small change jingles in my pocket. I hold my hand against it. There you are. Now it's happened. Just as I expected. How on earth has she managed to lose him? What a fool she is! No, I don't want Vanya to disappear now. Later perhaps, but not now. We have unfinished business, and the premiere, I haven't made it up to him yet for yesterday's quarrel.

Masha is waiting on Tverskaya Street.

"What happened?"

"We had the haircut, went shopping, bought everything – jeans, a shirt (a very nice one), went into a cafe to celebrate, I went to the toilet, and when I came back he wasn't there. What can we do?" Masha looks at me, frightened and completely vulnerable, like a naughty dog. "Where could he have gone?" she tries to sound positive in order to hide her desperation.

"How should I know!"

"Where can he be? What is he interested in?"

"He's unpredictable, damn it!"

"For some reason, after his haircut he gathered the hair up in a bag and put it in his pocket. Does that tell us anything?"

"He always does that."

"But what for?"

"What does it matter?" I'm annoyed. This is a fine time for questions like that.

"Perhaps it'll help us to find him," Masha says apologetically.

"He collects his hair because he believes that if a stranger gets it they might put the evil eye on him."

"The evil eye?"

"A hex, a bad spell."

"I see."

"Or the cleaner in the barber's shop will swear while he is sweeping up the hair and bring bad energy on him. Or some birds might make nests out of his hair and shit in it. It would be like them shitting on his head."

Masha smiles. I can't help smiling too.

"Well, did that information help?"

"He may just have gone home."

"Home?" How odd that didn't occur to us straight away.

"Does he have keys?"

"Yes, he wears them round his neck."

Masha and I rush to the metro.

The apartment door is locked and there is no one inside. I check Vanya's hiding place. It's empty. There is nothing in the large pocket.

"The painting isn't there. He must have taken it and gone somewhere."

"Perhaps he decided to give it back?"

"He doesn't want to give it back. Do you still not understand that? And tell your sister she'll get fuck all from us now, if not less!"

Masha is silent.

"He'd already hidden it somewhere else," I remember. "When Sonya burst in and shook him, the painting was already not here."

"He wouldn't go just anywhere. Think. The dacha? The cemetery?" Masha lists the options.

***

Half an hour later, we race through the cemetery gate. It is already getting dark. There are wet leaves underfoot. There are old gravestones, new monuments, moss-covered fences. Here is Plot 49B, the turning, the well... Oh, thank God!

"Vanya, what are you doing?" We squeeze past the pilot's railings. Vanya is wielding a shovel. My parents' urns lie at his feet like mortar shells. The grave has been half excavated.

"Vanya, are you crazy! What the hell are you doing?" I snatch the shovel out of his hands.

"Dad, don't swear. I decided to dig up the artist," Vanya replies calmly and confidently.

"Why? What use is he to you?"

"My angel told me he has been resurrected in the coffin. I need to let him out."

"How could such a thing possibly come into your head! Digging up a grave! It's a crime! It's completely insane, Vanya!" He hears me out without interrupting.

"The angel told me to."

"Your angel, your f...!" I manage to swallow the swearword itching to leave my lips. "Thank God no one noticed or we'd be looking for you and your angel in the loony bins of Moscow!"

Vanya is standing knee-deep in the grave. His new navy blue corduroy trousers are smeared with clay. His cranberry red shirt is unbuttoned, but his haircut is snazzy, his temples clean-shaven, his hair sticking up like a cockscomb.

"Where did you get the shovel?"

"Over there." Vanya gestures indefinitely. "They're repairing the road and there was a shovel."

"You have a distinct streak of kleptomania."

"I'll give it back."

I remember the Petroleum Venus.

"Did you decide to dig him up and hide the picture here?"

Vanya gives me a distinctly judgmental look, as if he has twigged that I've been rummaging through his hiding place without permission. His expression becomes stony. Although it is him standing in the pit and looking up, I feel I am at his feet. He proclaims proudly, "I have hidden the painting elsewhere."

We can hear the wind whistling in the branches of the trees. Far away, behind the cemetery walls, the city is buzzing.

"How do you like Vanya's new image?" Masha breaks the silence. "I think the colours go well. And the hairstyle."

Vanya draws himself up in the pit to his full height. Filling the grave back in any old how, we depart. We can only lean the shovel against the lodge. Vanya has forgotten quite where and from whom he borrowed it.

***

On the day of the premiere, 24 December, I came to my senses and decided to wash my clothes in order to look my best too. Vanya, who customarily did the laundry, loaded the clothes into the washing machine, meticulously weighing them beforehand. ("They had to weigh not more than five kilograms.") Throughout the program, he watched the drum rotating. He had me watching the spectacle too. I love watching the sheets and towels falling on top of each other as they spin behind the round glass door. When the drum stops for soaking, you can recognize some of the items in the general pile of wet rags. Then Vanya gleefully yells that here's his shirt, and there's my sock. The water pours in, splashing against our porthole-door and our ship seems to be sinking. The drum speeds up, pumping out the water, and the laundry is plastered against it by centrifugal force, revealing the shiny wall at the back.

It used to be that the grey, goffered hose to drain off the dirty water discharged directly into the sink. It was attached to the tap with a ribbon from a cake box. The hose would stiffen erotically before ejaculating a powerful, turbid jet of yellowish-grey liquid. If I was nearby at such moments, I contemplated that stream, happy in the knowledge that this was dirt of which my clothes were now free. When it had finished its business, the hose became flaccid until it was time for its next discharge. Nowadays, though, the hose empties directly into the drains and I can no longer enjoy watching the jet of murky water, or share the hose's cycle of pleasurable tension and release.

I entrusted Vanya with hanging out my washing on the balcony, and he promptly dropped my best jeans over the edge. I should have been able just to run down to the courtyard, pick them off the ground, and be done with it, but no such luck. The jeans snagged at fourth floor level on the branches of an aspen tree. Too bad the balcony didn't look out on the side of the house which had the advertisement hung over it. Then my jeans wouldn't have been hanging on a tree.

Vanya and I stood in silence on the balcony, like sailors looking out over waves into which they have just consigned their comrades' coffins. I mentally bade my jeans farewell. The tree was too far from the side of the house for me to reach it with a stick out of a window. Climbing was too dangerous because the upper branches were thin; and it would be too expensive to come to an arrangement with a builder. We would just have to admire the jeans till the end of our days, and wear a different pair in the meantime. As it happened, those were the only stylish, expensive jeans I possessed.

I thought I might be able to exploit the fact that Vanya was feeling guilty to find out where he'd moved the painting to.

"It's a secret."

"Vanya, I won't mind about the jeans if you tell me. Deal?"

"You will have to forgive me, I am unable to tell you."

If we gave Lena the painting back, I might be able to take up with her again. I'd like that.

"Don't try to talk me round, Dad. I am a rock."

Growling something under my breath, I left the balcony.

***

The mirror in the hallway is distorted at Vanya's level, which makes his face look funny. He put on the cranberry-red shirt Masha had given him together with a watermelon-coloured jacket and was now straightening the folds.

"Have you got the invitations?"

He rummaged in his pockets. "No."

"Where are they? I'll take them."

"I don't know."

"What do you mean, you don't know? I gave them to you."

We began a search for the invitations. Where on earth had he put them?

"Vanya, try to think where you saw them last."

He ran red-faced from one room to another, turning over books and everything else. He looked under the bed. To no avail.

"Found one! You're a goof-ball."

I extracted a glossy square of paper from a pile of photos Vanya had dumped on his chair a few days ago to sort for an album.

"We've got one. Now to find the other."

Vanya returned to the mirror while I leafed through the photographs. Despite my best endeavours, no second invitation.

"Vanya, where's the other one?"

"Isn't it there?"

"See for yourself."

Further searching proved fruitless. I moved all the photos off the armchair and sat down. "One, two three, four, five..." I counted mentally, to keep myself from physically assaulting Vanya. He looked at me helplessly.

"What are we going to do?"

"Give the invitation to Sonya and Masha and stay at home. You can't first invite someone and then cancel the invitation!"

He hung his head. I took a cigarette and lit it.

"You shouldn't smoke indoors," Vanya mentioned timidly.

"Don't make me angry…"

I smoked, drumming my fingers restlessly on the plush arm of Vanya's chair. This was a fiasco, a complete and utter fiasco! I wouldn't get to see Lena. I hadn't got her phone number. The feel of the plush relaxed me. I was enjoying stroking the velvety nap. My fingers slipped down between the arm and the seat cushion. I felt clumps of dust, sand, something cold. I extracted a rouble coin and shoved my hand back into the soft crevice to finger my way along every inch. There it was! Even before I pulled out my find, I knew exactly what I had in my grasp. Now, though, the newly found invitation was not enough. I was possessed by the mania of the treasure hunter. With both hands I delved into every nook behind the cushions and found more treasure: an old lipstick. I twisted out the red cylinder. It was worn down almost to the base. My heart leaped as I realized that was the very first lipstick I ever came across. When I was three or four, I noticed where my mother put the bright object she rubbed on her lips. Waiting for the right moment, I seized the case, twisted out the brand new bar with its generic slant, and took a bite. That must have been my first big disappointment in life. Instead of the sweetness promised by its bright gleam, my tongue tasted some greasy, yukky stuff with a chemical smell. My teeth stuck in as if it were toffee.

I showed off my finds to Vanya. "So we can go again?"

"Yes."

"Then I want to put the lipstick on my lips," he said for no apparent reason. I was dumbfounded.

"Why?"

"In the theatre we had our lips, and eyes, and cheeks painted. It's called makeup. We're going to the cinema and they use makeup there too."

"In the theatre you were an actor, but we are going to the cinema to be in the audience."

"The audience? That's okay. I don't like painting my eyes and cheeks, but I want to paint my lips."

I didn't argue. After all, what's so unusual about boys wearing lipstick?

"Only, please, not too much!"

Vanya puckered his lips, as if for a kiss.

"No, the other way. You have to stretch them. Like this." I stretched my lips. Vanya followed suit. "And you're telling me they painted your lips?" I passed the lipstick lightly over his lips and rub it in. He looked at himself in the mirror.

"That's nice! Put some more on!"

"It might look a bit odd."

"I want more!"

I had to paint his lips fairly boldly, and then I noticed a single hair sprouting on his chin. I gave it a playful tug.

"It's time to buy you a razor! You're a real man now."

Vanya examined the hair in the mirror, forgetting about his lips. "Will I shave like you, Dad?"

"Just like me. And I'll shave just like you!" I slapped him man-to-man on the shoulder.

"Keep painting. You're not concentrating," Vanya complained, remembering his lips. I applied the lipstick even more thickly.

"That's good now," Vanya decided, after inspecting his improbably lurid mouth with satisfaction.

***

In the courtyard, the sisters were waiting. I offered to drive for Sonya. "You drive all the time. Have a drink, take it easy. I'll do the driving."

"No. I'm not going to be drinking anyway."

"Why not?"

"I'm on antibiotics. Let's get going. Only, some dumbcluck in an X5 drove into me and the door's stuck. Who wants to climb in through the window?" Sonya asked, starting the engine.

"Can I?" Vanya asked shyly. "I would like to climb in through the window!"

Sonya lowered the side window and, while Masha and I settled ourselves in the back seat, Vanya, floundering, tumbled in through the off-roader's window on to the passenger seat. First, his top appeared. Then he got stuck and had to ask for help. Sonya grabbed him by the scruff of the neck and the next moment, with his head on the carpet and his legs on the leather seat, he was entirely in the car. Vanya managed to restore his legs and head to a more traditional position only when we were already crossing Novoarbat Bridge.

We didn't speak. Why was she taking antibiotics? My mind immediately went back to our unprotected sex. Did the antibiotics indicate that Sonya had found she was infected with something? A venereal disease, for instance? Which she might have passed on to me?

Sonya executed another of her dazzling driving manoeuvres, leaving me with my nose buried in the chinchilla collar of Masha's coat. The fur was soft and slightly damp. It was drizzling in the streets. I put my hand down on the seat to steady myself. Masha's was beside it. Our banking manoeuvre lasted just long enough for me to feel the softness of her cheek, to breathe in the fragrance of her hair, to feel the cold diamond in her ear. What if I had AIDS? I was being ridiculous; you don't treat AIDS with antibiotics. Masha's fingers and mine entwined. I casually removed my hand, as if to scratch.

Seeing a flower stall at the crossroads, Sonya slammed on the brakes. "We can't possibly arrive without flowers."

I was about to get out to do her bidding but, "No, Dad! I'll go!"

Without stopping to think whether it was better to stick his legs or his head out of the window first, Vanya somehow fell out of the car in a heap and ran to the stall. Passers-by and the flower-seller were surprised to see a small person emerge from a Jeep in this manner, but after a brief consultation with the florist, Vanya reappeared at the window.

"She's got tulips. Purple ones, pink ones, and... and... Oh, shit! I've forgotten!" Vanya hit the door with his hand and went back to the stall. 'Shit'? That was new.

"And there's also yellow with a fringe! There!"

"What about you? Which ones did you like best?" Sonya asked, rummaging in her purse.

"The purple ones, like Masha gave me at the theatre."

"Get thirty of them," Sonya said, holding out the money.

"No, no! I'll pay!" I protested.

"Just leave off, will you?"

"What does 'leave off' mean?"

"Your invitation, our flowers!"

After some toing and froing we agreed to pay half each.

The transparent box of the flower stall was like a glass full of a tropical cocktail. The windows were, predictably, misted up, and in among the sheaves of flowers you could see the shadows of Vanya and the florist moving.

"What's that on his lips?" Sonya asked.

"Yes, I was wondering too!" Masha echoed.

"He's put on lipstick."

"But why?"

"You can't just turn up to a premiere without your makeup on."

The sisters hooted with laughter.

But what if it was me? What if she'd picked up something from me, something which developed slowly which I didn't know about? It does happen. Men can have no symptoms, while women have real trouble.

Five minutes later, Vanya shoved a tight bunch of tulips through the window. The car was filled with sturdy, crunching stems and the fresh fragrance of closed, drop-shaped buds.

"I'm going to be shaving soon! Like Dad!"

***

The cars in front of the cinema were like puppies huddling to get at their mother's nipples. Immediately after the metal detector, there was a semi-circle of press photographers, and beyond them the guests. Elderly ladies with big handbags; girls with long legs sprouting out of micro-dresses; some hairy, bearded types, probably members of the film crew; wealthy men with cigars and tight-fitting pink shirts over their muscled bodies, probably friends of the producers. I saw a few faces from my past life and nodded to someone.

"Hello, Fyodor!"

"Irina!" It was the clairvoyant, wearing a necklace of large amber beads, arm in arm with a man.

"Let me introduce you to my husband, Pavel."

"We've already... Oh, delighted to meet you, Pavel." I shake his wrinkled hand and wonder if he's recognized me. He somehow looks as if he hadn't had enough sleep.

"A friend gave me her invitation. She worked for them as a makeup artist," the medium says. "How did you get on? Have you found the owners of the painting?"

"Oh, yes, actually we have."

"It's going to be sunny tomorrow." Irina remarks,

looking closely first at Vanya, and then at me. Because of the lipstick, I imagine.

"Wow, really? Thank you!" Vanya says delightedly.

"Thank me for what? It's nothing to do with me. It's fate."

Lena! I feel I want to disappear, to hide somewhere. With two enchanting children, a girl of about ten and a boy a bit younger.

"Hey! I'm so glad you came!"

"Sonya, Masha, this is Lena…"

The sisters exchange a glance, probably beginning to suspect how Lena and I are related. She discreetly takes a close look at Vanya.

"This is Vanya. Vanya this is Lena."

"Delighted to meet you," Vanya says, kissing her hand and bowing in his own special way. He leaves the red imprint of his lips on her hand. I surreptitiously watch her. Something changes in her expression for an instant, like that dry sprig of parsley caught by the water in the sink.

"This is Dasha, Sergey's daughter," Lena tells us, patting the girl on the head. "And this is Nikita. Ours." She hugs the boy, who looks down shyly. He is very smart in his little suit and resembles his mother. So does Vanya, but what a difference there is in how they look like her, Vanya and little Nikita. Identical mechanisms but manufactured in different factories, one licensed, the other a pirate enterprise.

"Go on through to the auditorium. I have to go on stage now. They'll be introducing the production team. See you at the reception!"

I give Vanya a sign but he doesn't understand. I wink meaningfully. Vanya asks Lena, "I look pretty cool in this gear, don't I?"

"Yes, it's very stylish."

"I'll be shaving soon. See?" Vanya feels for the hair on his chin and shows it off. "Vanya, the flowers…" I point to the bouquet.

Vanya remembers the tulips and gives them to Lena.

***

After the words of welcome and expressions of gratitude, the screening begins. This is a real musical, with long dance routines and vocal numbers. It is the tale of Alyonushka, a poor girl, but pretty and honest. Her neighbours and friends envy her intelligence and beauty, and one day they give her a poisoned apple. Alyonushka takes an antidote, makes short shrift of the evil-doers, and heads off with the most eligible suitor. Some people help her, and wild animals, and the ancient spirits of the land, which give her oil. Curiously enough, all the good characters are blond and all the bad people have dark hair and wear glasses.

The best scene is the finale, – festivities in a forest glade. In the middle is a circle surrounded by the battlements of a fortress resembling those of the Kremlin, only made of ice. From behind some slender birch trees comes a score of boys and girls in gaily embroidered folk costumes. The boys have balalaikas, form a line in front of the fortress, and strike up the slow, lyrical opening bars of "Kalinka".

Alack, beneath the pine tree, 'neath the tall,

green pine tree

Take my poor bones and lay me there to rest.
Ai, lyuli-lyuli; ai, lyuli-lyuli
Take my poor bones and lay me there to-oo-oo rest!

The singers divide to reveal five figures with red cloaks inside the circle. Their cloaks fall to the ground. Three are girls: one mulatto, another a brunette with the painted eyes of an ancient Egyptian, and the third is blonde Alyonushka.

The girls wear lingerie painted with yellow folk art leaves and red berries. Alyonushka too is in bra and panties, only hers are golden. The girls are all wearing red stiletto heels and clasping in their hands bottles of vodka named after the president. (The film's main sponsor is a distillery.) The two others are boys wearing vests and combat trousers. Their Adidas trainers are navy blue, with the emblematic three white stripes. They carry whips and have their biceps tattooed with helicopters, tanks, and paratroopers. They are suntanned and athletic, their faces hidden by special-operations face masks.

Ka-linka, Kalinka, Kalinka, my love!
Little berry in my orchard, my orchard, my love!

At first, singing their folk song of snowberries and raspberries, five lithe bodies smoothly circle each other, like animals in a courtship ritual. Then the mixed race girl puts a vodka bottle on her head and her hands on her hips. One boy cracks his whip, wrapping the lash round the bottle. A flick, a tug, and he holds it in his hands, the girl unharmed, the bottle intact. The audience whistles and claps appreciatively.

The second boy repeats the trick no less adroitly, but with the brunette.

Kalinka, Malinka, Malinka, my love!

The boys start moving in on Alyonushka from both sides. She puts a bottle on her head. They crack their whips and snare the glistening bottle at exactly the same moment. Lena-Alyonushka jumps back as their eyes bore into each other with theatrical menace. Each has a bottle in his left hand, while the third is held quivering in mid-air by the tensed whips.

Oh, my green, my tall green pine tree
Still now your ne-e-edles above my grave!

The boys begin rhythmically rocking their entwined whips and the bottle.

Ai, lyuli-lyuli-i-iii
Still now your le-e-eaves above my grave!
Ka-a-a-a…, the choir sings, poised...

The boys dash the bottle to the ground. Splintering glass, spurting vodka.

Kalinka, Malinka, Malinka, my love!

As if on cue, the boys dash the bottles they are holding against their foreheads and computer graphics transfigure the splinters and splashes into seams of diamonds.

I turn to look at Vanya. He is watching, transfixed.

One of the dancers whistles and the boys tear off their hats and masks to reveal the heads of The Wolf and The Bear. The animal heads grow naturally on their human bodies. Their snout-faces express human emotion, smiling, baring their fangs. Wolf's top left fang is gold.

The singers in the chorus also throw off their clothes and begin dancing wildly. Close-ups alternate with wide shots, angled from above and below. The dancers perform everything expected in a Russian folk dance and more. The girls turn cartwheels, do high kicks and hand stands. Wolf dances on his hunkers, leaping high, spreading his legs wide, his hands touching the tips of his trainers. Bear jumps head over heels again and again.

Great raindrops fall from the skies, black drops on Alyonushka's face, more and more of them. The dancers strip off their painted bras, only Lena-Alyonushka remains covered. The boy-beasts are magically stripped to black shorts. "Kalinka" rings out in a cutting-edge electronic rendition, its tight rhythm like the beating of one big communal heart.

Kalinka, Malinka, Malinka, my love!

"Oil, oil, oil, oil," hammers through the hall.

Sure enough, it is raining oil, which the Mother Spirit

of the Earth has bestowed upon Alyonushka. It becomes a downpour. The dancers whirl insanely beneath it. Muscles bulge on shoulders, calves, and bellies. The girls' hair sprays black wetness over the screen, a wetness which can enable you to travel at fantastic speed, to fly round the globe in a day, erect skyscrapers, roll out a banquet, or hold on to power and make it grow.

OIL!

Glimpses of animal snouts flecked with gold, female breasts, birch trees. From the heavens, black gold pours down. No, this dance is dedicated not just to oil. It is dedicated to all of us, to all of Russia. Khokhloma folk art and oil. Ice and suntan. Striptease and whirling folk dances.

New Russia has merged with Eternal Russia. Behold my country, the great enigma, where everything is as precarious as the electricity supply of a house which mainly depends on a mobile diesel generator. If the generator packs in, it's the end of everything, but until it does we won't build a power station. We'll keep our fingers crossed.

Behold my Russia, a flighty madam accustomed to money and men dancing attendance on her. Everyone knows she is coarse and vulgar, drinks too much, behaves abominably, but she has only to smile for everyone to forgive her. Just that tender smile, that gaze straight into your eyes, and you are sunk, no longer responsible for your actions. My homeland whose every act is unpredictable. Today, dressed to kill, enticing, billing and cooing; and tomorrow she will throw on a stained, crumpled vest, open the door, fold her arms to hide the punctured veins, push you out and pretend she never knew you. If she wants, she will spit in your face; if she wants, she will give herself to you.

Feet tap in time to the music. Some of the audience are dancing in the aisles. The images of the film get mixed in with the kaleidoscope of my visions. My country, whooping and cheering, rushes past in front of me. Sailors trashing palaces, and aristocratic young ladies flirting at their first ball; "grandad" conscripts in the army beating up the greenhorns, and drunken merchants hurtling around Moscow in their sleighs; Cossacks in earrings slash with sabres, Jewish violins lament, horses hauling cannons sink in mud, bears dance at fairs, headscarves whirl like the wind, leaders of peasant revolts are caged in Red Square, fingers of secret policemen squeeze triggers, political prisoners fell timber.

There are the fascists' nooses from which Young Communist martyrs dangle, and here are the fascists themselves on their way to be shot, goose-stepping, arms outstretched in a final salute. Here are the priests with a pentagram branded on their foreheads. Here are drunken women in pink, fur-trimmed anoraks dancing in front of the Lenin Mausoleum on New Year's Eve. Here are the agents of Smersh in their dark blue breeches shooting in the back condemned men fighting in war-time penal battalions. Black-eyed mountain-dwellers cut the throats of yesterday's schoolboys from Ryazan or Tambov, freshly kitted out in Russian military uniform. Slit-eyed horsemen, blond-bearded Slav warriors.

On the screen, the dancers' bodies merge to form strange hydra-headed creatures with multiple arms and legs. Chortling, antic faces.

My nose is tingling. I unobtrusively wipe tears from my eyes. It's only love. I love this whole appalling shambles. I am a part of it. I don't need any order beyond this chaos, beyond this indefinableness. Thank you, Russia, for the passion, for the atrocities, for your charm, for our suffering.

Witches fly in mortars and on mops, mermaids frolic

beneath the vaults of sunken bell towers, a troika of black steeds drags gun carriages spraying machine-gun fire. The world is blessed by the cross tattooed on a convict's back. And above it all there sits in glory – He, the Eternal Joker, the Artist who created me, and Vanya, and the Petroleum Venus.

I see the audience through the eyes of the characters in the film. I see the film through the eyes of the audience. I see the whole world through the eyes of surveillance cameras. Skyscrapers, blue domes studded with golden stars, nuclear submarines, a hail of arrows tipped with flaming resin. Malachite, the rack, boyar noblemen, princes torn to pieces, space rockets. The birch twig switches in bathhouses fuse with rods lashing bloodied backs. The steam pouring out of the bathhouse goes up the chimneys of thermal power plants. Camps, forests, distant horizons. The haze over black rivers, over marshes at the bottom of which lie chests full of the treasure foreigners have tried to haul away. Nearby lie the foreigners' remains and, beside them, those of the defenders.

***

When the lights came up in the auditorium, I put on a determined smile and hid my eyes to conceal my tears. We followed everybody else into the hall where tables of food were waiting.

"Well, Vanya, did you enjoy the musical?"

"I enjoyed it very much. I like it when everybody is dancing and singing!"

After filling a plate, we leaned against a pillar and tucked in to prawn sushi. Vanya had never tasted it. My mother believed that if you ate the tiniest piece of raw fish you were guaranteed to end up with a six-metre tapeworm in your gut. Sonya and Masha spotted some friends and went off to chat with them.

"I really like these round things," Vanya mumbled through a mouthful of sushi.

"I'll get some more," I said, leaving him by the pillar. The snacks had temporarily run out and I had to wait for the waiter to bring a new supply. When I got back to Vanya, I found him in the company of three tipsy gentlemen of various ages. The oldest, a gloomy bearded character, looked to be about fifty. The middle one was a bespectacled man of about my own age, and the youngest a black-haired man in his early twenties with Asiatic features. I arrived back just as the gloomy one was pressing a full glass of vodka on Vanya.

"Thank you, but I do not drink," Vanya declined firmly. "It spoils your karma."

"He doesn't drink. He has a weak heart!" I interrupted, making it very clear that Vanya was under my protection.

"He can drink to Russia! After a film like that!" my bespectacled peer contradicted loudly.

I inspected him: a fair-haired intellectual, probably a journalist, or a film critic. "I will drink to Russia with you." They poured me a glass.

"You've drunk enough to Russia already, Misha," the gloomy character told the intellectual.

"What's come over you, Boris? Hail to Russia!" With these words, the intellectual flung out his arm in a nazi salute.

"Christ Almighty! It's people like you are going to bring the whole fucking show down on top of us!" the beardy swore, and downed his vodka on his own. The young Asian drank in silence. All the swearing frightened Vanya. I patted his shoulder and gave him the plate of prawn rolls to calm him down. The fascistically inclined intellectual was the last to drink; he grunted, and again extolled Russia.

"What's so great about fucking Russia? Any time now everything's going to go arse over tit! It's time to get out! I'm not going to wait for revolutionary sailors to come and break the door down. I've had enough!" the beardy continued, his hot breath redolent of expensive vodka.

"People need to pay their taxes so the state will be strong," the young Asian muttered, looking resentful.

"You know, Renat, our parents paid this country all it's owed for centuries to come!"

"Not 'this' country but 'our' country!" the Tatar patriot of Russia rounded on him.

"I worked for the Administration for ten years, so kindly don't argue about my relationship with 'your' country!" the older man replied darkly, before pouring us all more vodka.

"So, how did your parents pay Russia?" the intellectual challenged him, looking up through misted spectacles.

"They paid with the war!"

The beardy handed a glass to the intellectual.

"With the labour camps!"

A glass to the Tatar.

"With collectivization!"

I took the glass he offered.

"With the famine!"

He held out a glass to Vanya, but remembered himself and instead shoved it into the hand of a passing dandy from the Caucasus.

"With serfdom! What taxes do we owe after all that?" We drank.

"Hail to Russia!" the intellectual shouted, before his head slumped down.

"Well, what do you have to say?" the gloomy man with

the dark beard turned to me. "Me?" I'd been hoping to get by without being interrogated. "I, er…" I really don't like all this empty talk about the Destiny of Our Motherland. "I somehow just accept what happens. I like it all... I suppose I sort of put my trust in life, something like that."

"He accepts it! He likes it! Hah! The Zen of the doomed! How can you trust life when everybody here is like you! Nobody knows anything. Nobody thinks about the future! And anyway, what's the point in thinking if you're going to have everything taken off you? We haven't succeeded in changing a thing. The Russian people like being trounced. The tsars have always slaughtered their people. Ivan the Terrible was responsible for three massacres in Novgorod alone! He slaughtered his own, Russian people! Not even the Tatar dogs got that far... Oh, sorry, Renat." Beardy slapped the Tatar on the shoulder. "But Ivan the Terrible, the bastard, he managed it!"

"The Tatars got stuck in the mud, my dad told me," Vanya confirmed.

On to a nearby table, laden with empty glasses and plates of half-eaten canapes, clambered a frisky man with a paunch and a flushed Irina. Had her husband fallen asleep again? The couple began dancing, tightly pressed against each other. With every movement, something fell to the floor.

"Look around. This is truly a feast in time of plague!"

"Hail to Russia!" the intellectual exclaimed, waving his arms.

"Misha, have you been drinking on your own?" the gloomy man asked the intellectual with an unexpectedly gentle smile.

The young Tatar refilled the glasses. One of the clean-shaven musclemen in bright shirts came over to us, except that this one had a beard.

"Talking politics again?" he asked squeamishly.

"Yes, Holy Father, what else!"

"Meet Father Anatoly, a man of the cloth who thinks like us," the gloomy orator introduced the newcomer.

"Admit you prefer the Catholics!" the bespectacled intellectual accused Father Anatoly in an inquisitorial voice.

Father Anatoly looked with ostentatious contempt around the room, at Irina dancing on the table and her partner whispering sweet nothings in her ear, and said gravely, "If we were Catholics, there would be none of this mess going on."

"Verily, verily, my dealer says the same!" the intellectual shouted. "Join us for a drink?"

"Misha, you know I have kidney trouble; and in any case the astrologer warned me against it."

"Russia needs a firm hand," the young Tatar said to nobody in particular.

"Well, young fellow, you belong to the next generation, how are you planning to survive in this accursed country?" the beardy enquired gloomily.

"I'm studying at the police academy precisely so that I can somehow have a life here. In a police state you have to stick to the authorities to have any prospects. You stand no chance of making a lot of money unless you work for secret services," the young man recited, as if reading a text, as if he hadn't been getting plastered all this time but preparing his speech.

"So you young people have no desire to change anything? Are you going to take bribes and all that?"

"I'm only going to take large bribes." The guy was evidently one of those who, by the time they are twenty, have their lives clearly mapped out for the next sixty years.

The beardy waved his hands in front of his face after

the fashion of a soothsayer: "I see the Kremlin and the oligarchs' estates in Rublyovka in flames! I do not want to be among those crazed hordes. I want to be sitting in my private villa in Cannes, tasting cheeses, drinking wine, and watching everything here go up in flames on television! We are sailing on the Titanic and it's time to man the lifeboats!"

"A satanic country!" Father Anatoly concurred, pursing his lips. "Boris, pour me a drink."

We drank. Someone touched my arm. I turned to find Sonya and Masha in front of me. Broken glass and oyster shells crunched beneath their heels. The beardy came to life:

"Girls, forgive my importunity. We are in the middle of a debate. Tell me, why does Russia have all these problems?"

"What problems?" Sonya asked.

"Well, these…" The drink was beginning to deprive the beardy of his rhetorical skills. He just gestured towards the room at large. Under the feet of the couple dancing on the table, a dish of leftover delicacies crashed to the floor. Vanya looked at me anxiously. I gave him a reassuring pat.

"It's because you didn't surrender to the French when you had the chance," Masha explained, beating her sister to the draw.

It seemed as if everybody had come today prepared to talk politics. When Russians get drunk they immediately start talking about politics and the war, as if those were the only topics possible. Masha's pronouncement had the effect of waking up all present. Even the vertically challenged intellectual looked up and asked, "Whassat you s-say?"

"You should have surrendered to the French in 1812. Can you imagine what you would have here today? The great culture of Russia would have been sanctified by the great culture of France. You would have parks, foie gras, an

Eiffel Tower, a Montmartre. At the very least, you'd have French passports and wouldn't be crowding for visas."

"So you really think it was all the fault of Kutuzov?" Sonya asked, genuinely surprised.

"Of General Frost and Kutuzov!" Masha replied emphatically.

"If I had to surrender, I'd be happy to surrender to you," the beardy declared with brazen aplomb.

"I take no prisoners," Masha retorted. I saw her through new eyes. Her cheeks were burning. She was flying, talking with no accent.

"Even though you didn't surrender to the French, destiny gave you a second chance with the Germans. You really should have surrendered to the Germans. Hitler, incidentally, was intending to make a sea near Moscow! Not even Luzhkov managed to make you a sea! At least you'd have a sea now! The Germans, of course, are not the French, but at least they would have made everything neat and tidy."

"That is so absolutely true!" the Tatar student of the police academy suddenly contributed.

"Don't interrupt," the beardy chided him. "Please continue."

"Russia is like a capricious bride who sends all her good suitors packing until no one will take her. Who are you holding out for? The Americans? The Chinese?"

"We mustn't surrender to the Chinese. They eat dogs!" Vanya interjected with great concern.

"It's the Koreans eat dogs!"

"In short, all your problems stem from your inability to make the most of your opportunities," concluded Maria-Letizia-Geneviève, Paris Silver Medalist in Under-21s Kickboxing.

"I do have one idea on this topic," said the student of the

police academy. "I recently read a classified translation of Nostradamus. It said there that Europe will suffer a terrible catastrophe in 2012. Earthquakes, floods, and droughts. Half of Italy will sink and Spain will be wiped out by forest fires. On top of all that, there will be a war. The Arabs will start slaughtering white people. There will be complete chaos, but Moscow will not be affected. Then all the Europeans will come clammering to us from their devastated lands. That would be the ideal time to surrender to them, to all of them at once, to the Germans and the French, and even to the Baltic!"

A waiter walked by with a tray laden with glasses. "Maitre! Wine for the ladies!" Masha took a glass.

"I'm only going to surrender to the Italians," Father Anatoly giggled.

The man dancing on the table tripped and fell to the floor with a great crash.

"Oleg, are you all right?" Irina shouted, laughing. Oleg was unharmed. Getting to his feet, he brushed prawn tails from his clothing and proffered a hand to Irina. She descended to him with all the grace a 100-kilogram drunk lady could muster.

"If you surrender to the French, nothing will change," Vanya objected timidly, returning to the interrupted conversation. Everybody turned to give him the kind of look reserved for someone who resuscitates a topic they are already bored with and were forgetting.

"What do you mean, nothing will change, young man? They will impart their culture to us, their experience and traditions."

"No one will be able to change Russia. Rus..." Vanya was becoming flustered. "Wussia will change evwybody elth. In Wussia, evwybody will become Wussian."

There was a perplexed silence. All around was the background noise of music and voices, but it seemed to us like silence.

"Well, thank God for that!" Everybody raised their vodka and wine glasses and clinked with Vanya, who was holding a tumbler of fruit juice.

"Hail to Russia!"

***

I saw Lena and she beckoned me over.

"Here, this is for you and Vanya for the holidays." She slipped me something wrapped in an advertisement.

"I didn't bring him so... Thank you... It's just... Well, you know."

"It's okay. He's looking very good. How are your parents?"

"They've died."

"Oh, I'm sorry."

"And yours?"

"My father's in Switzerland getting treatment for his back and my mother is with him. Well, I must dash."

"Hey... What are you doing over the holiday? We could meet up."

"I'll be abroad."

She was gone. I opened a corner of the wrapper. It was money. I shoved it in my pocket. The guys I'd been talking to came by, dragging the bespectacled intellectual by his arms.

"Hail to Russia..." I heard him murmur.

"Misha, shut the fuck up! You need to sleep this off."

"Pile him into my car. I'll cart him home," I heard the Tatar say.

I went back to Vanya and the sisters. "Home?"

We go out into the damp coolness of the street. "Get in. We'll take you back," Sonya offers.

"That is my favourite song," Vanya suddenly announces.

"What is?"

"Kalinka-Malinka, my love."

Ahead of us, skyscrapers are under construction. They look like vast ships sinking perpendicularly into the ground. On one of the cranes a broad Russian tricolor flaps and flutters. There is a spotlight on the top of the tallest skyscraper. Its powerful white beam probes the sky. Just like when I was at the dacha, except that my torch beam was puny while this one lights up the clouds, as if there is an air raid. What a waste of good money. Or maybe it's not just for effect? Maybe the people up there in the skyscraper also want to talk to God. They've invested all that money in order to climb higher. They've installed a powerful searchlight... "Hey, God!" For miles in every direction the dormitory suburbs extend, and here in this high tower priests are tirelessly trying to find even the slightest hint in the sky. Even the slightest hope.

***

Back home, we said our goodbyes.

"Thanks for the evening."

"Come to our birthdays!" Vanya invited them.

"Absolutely! Your birthdays are next to each other in late December, right?"

"Actually, mine is the day after tomorrow. That is, tomorrow, and…," I began.

"And mine is the day after the day after tomorrow, that is, the day after the day after…" Vanya got in a tangle.

"We'll be there."

Sonya called me aside.

"Oooh, secrets!" Masha exclaimed.

"No, of course not. I saw you getting along well with that actress."

"We are old friends."

"I understand. Did you tell her about the picture?"

"I'm going to."

"Don't put it off, or I'll tell them myself you've got the painting. I can do without other people's problems. Well, so long for now." Sonya got back into the Jeep.

In front of our entry, in a bed of forget-me-nots which were flowering out of season, Vanya spotted something and bent down. Another of his finds. This time it was a padlock with the key sticking out of it.

"That's a useful thing," he decided.

"I expect it's rusty."

Vanya turned the key with some effort and the hasp clicked open. "It works!"

"Congratulations."

"Dad, if it was locked, does that mean it was locking someone in?"

"It was just lying there. It wasn't locking anyone in. Someone has lost it."

"No, it was locking someone in! Someone invisible... or some thing." Vanya really loves mystery. "And now I've set it free."

"Well, perhaps that's right. You know best," I said, ruffling my son's hair.

As we were going in, our excited caretaker rushed out to meet us. "Your downstairs neighbour's apartment is all flooded! It's poor Taisiya Petrovna! The pipe must be blocked and we can only get it cleared from your apartment. Quick! She's already talking about calling out an emergency team!"

We ran upstairs. When you are met with news like

that, there's no telling what state you are going to find your apartment in. By the door, two workmen in overalls smelling of cigarette smoke were hard at work, watched by Taisiya Petrovna, the devout widow of a former Soviet deputy minister of defence. The plumber was Russian, with the deep wrinkles of a heavy drinker and metal teeth. His apprentice was a young Caucasian who was dragging around a long ribbed steel hose with a knob on the end.

"Oh, at last! I'm quite worn out! Let us in, quickly!" Taisiya Petrovna wailed, tugging at her dyed tresses, which were in curlers.

"The access eye is located on your premises. We have to rod from there."

"The what?" I asked uncomprehendingly.

"The cleanout pipe! It's specially for unblocking the stack."

"Oh, please let them in!" Taisiya Petrovna implored, pulling a curler out of her hair and wiping her mouth with it, evidently taking it for a handkerchief. Real ladies register anxiety by raising a handkerchief to their lips, and what widow of a former Soviet deputy minister of defence, even a devout one, does not aspire to be a lady?

"The people in the apartment above mine keep emptying water down the drain. For some reason they've taken it into their heads to wash their dishes in the middle of the night! If the pipe is blocked it all comes up in my sink. I can't bail it out fast enough!"

"Of course. Go on in."

Their heavy boots echoing on the parquet, the plumbers went through to the kitchen. The foreman pointed to an inconspicuous cap mounted on the waste pipe. Like the pipe itself, it was covered in many layers of gloss paint. I couldn't remember it ever having been opened.

"We'll just get these bolts off, remove the hatch, and unblock the stack."

"Go ahead."

The plumber got to work unfastening the bolts. Vanya came to watch too. As the last bolt was released, something unexpected happened. A short, violent fountain of stinking black fluid spurted out of the hatch, spraying everyone from head to toe. We looked like goggle-eyed chocolate covered marshmallows.

"Wot woz dat, Palych?" the startled apprentice asked, wiping the muck off his face.

"That, young fellow, was and is shit," the plumber pronounced gravely, popping with a callused finger a huge, iridescent black bubble which had formed in the hatch opening.

Having hastily rinsed myself off, I began cleaning up the floor and furniture. The plumbers thrust their hose with its knob into the hatch and began ramming it to and fro.

"Now! Now!" The blockage in the pipe was unyielding.

"Turn it on, Palych! Den it'll be stronger!" the young Caucasian puffed.

"Not yet!"

They rammed it forward again and again, the cable gradually penetrating more deeply. When all six metres of it had disappeared into the pipe, leaving only the end the workmen were holding, the plumber turned on the tap. The water in our sink still was not draining away.

"You've got your sink blocked as well!"

Vanya jumped up, looking decidedly uneasy. I was afraid there would be even more shit flying if he got a wallop on the ear from the heavy hose.

"Keep back, Vanya! The man will sort it out!"

The foreman had already unscrewed the U-bend and

pulled out a roll wrapped in a plastic bag. So that's where he hid it!

"Gimme!" Vanya grabbed the roll and hit me on the head with it.

"Vanya, what are you doing?"

"You want to take her away from me! You are bad!" Vanya belaboured me with the rolled-up Venus. I managed more or less to shield myself. The plumbers looked away.

"Vanya, stop it!" At that, he grabbed a frying pan out of the sink and whacked me hard on the side of the head.

***

I seem to see a sunny summer's day. I am at our dacha. I go over to the window. Vanya is standing on the grass, watering the flowers with a hose. He notices me and wickedly directs the hose at the window. The water bursts against the pane, divides, and runs down in streams behind which a sparkling Vanya is in fits of laughter.

I run out of the dacha. Vanya is not on the grass. I run behind the house to where the forest begins. From the trees, a strange creature emerges which looks like an elk, but without the antlers. It is magnificent, but not a stag; gentle, but not a hind. The creature stretches its funny, shaggy muzzle towards me and I stroke it, all the time wondering how it comes to be here. This area is all dachas, cars, people. How will it survive here? I can hardly take it home. Where would I put it?

The creature looks as if it knows what I am thinking, and I read in its eyes, "No need to blame yourself. It's all right." The creature gives me something like a parting smile and ambles back to the forest. I don't move. The sun dazzles me. I return to the present.

Everything around is unusually bright. There is no one

around. There are dried black blobs on the floor. My head is aching and I feel dizzy.

In Vanya's room I am blinded by brilliant sunlight. The solar orb is rising behind the houses across the river, behind the statues, the advertisement for stock cubes, the Ministry tower. A powerful shaft of yellow-white light fills the room and penetrates the remotest corners. For a moment my eyes cease to function and, blinded, I lower my head. Behind the closed eyelids a persistent gold circle bordered with green rotates on a metallic silvery background. When I can finally see again, I look about me. I stub my toe on the open padlock Vanya found outside the entrance. I swear, scowl, and clutch my foot.

The window is wide open. There is a big hole in the fabric of the advertisement. The bedclothes are in disarray. There is no sign of Vanya. He is not hiding behind the door, or under the bed, or in the cupboard. I really do not want to go near the window. Here is the window sill, the steel scaffolding, planking supported on crossbars, bolts.

My first memory of being alive is of sunlit commotion, dazzling light, my father throwing me up in the air. Many years later, I came across a photo which registered that moment. My mother is standing nearby with a strained smile on her lips, afraid my father may drop me. I am a chubby toddler with a big head flying upwards with an expression of sheer delight.

A sunbeam makes me blink. It is reflecting off a pair of scissors lying on the planking. I follow in Vanya's footsteps over the precarious boards. I hold on to an upright and look down.

I see the children's play area. Trees. Parked cars. The pavement. Vanya.

***

I run down the stairs, past the calendars with their pictures of birch trees and fluffy kittens, past the Virgin Mary and Jesus Christ. I run...

"How could he do that... why so suddenly... it wasn't supposed to be like this," I mutter under my breath, protesting to who knows whom.

"There's no hurry, it won't change anything... now I'm free... free... completely... perhaps I should just go somewhere and hide away from all this… burrow under the covers." I run down the stairs two at a time, slip, fall, run on, down and down.

On the ground floor I say hello to the caretaker. She is watching a morning comedy show on television.

There isn't a soul around. Where is everybody? Oh yes, it's Sunday. Everybody is still asleep.

Vanya is looking at the sky. He's got an allergic rash beginning near his lip. He shouldn't have eaten all those prawns yesterday. In his right hand he is clutching a twig with buds which are just about to open. He must have grabbed it as he was falling and is now clutching it tightly.

I raise my eyes. From earth to heaven I see a building-sized advertisement. The edges have eyelets laced with a cable, like a corset pulled tight. In the vicinity of Lena-Alyonushka's belly, up by our window, there is a gaping hole. A flap of the fabric is blowing in a light breeze we can't even feel down here. There is a white scar high up in the blue sky, traced by a plane.

***

The orderlies put Vanya on a black plastic sack. Not in it, on top of it. Perhaps it's a mark of respect. They don't want to turn my Vanya into "the body", the kind of trash which usually gets put in plastic sacks. I remember what Masha said about how afraid she was of seeing her Churchill in a sack like that.

"Tie the mouth shut or you won't be able to close it later," somebody advised me, and passed me a cloth. I tied Vanya's mouth shut. Yesterday's lipstick had dried and cracked. I didn't manage very well. The material kept slipping.

The ride in the ambulance was bumpy. "Either the road surface is bad or the shock absorbers have gone," I thought. They took Vanya from me at the mortuary. I just asked them to treat him gently, and not to take the twig out of his hand. "He doesn't like it when people take something away from him. He's a stubborn lad."

"What clothing is to be used?" the orderly asked briskly. Under his tunic I could see a bare chest with a few blond hairs. "Clothing?... I'll bring... Vanya has just had a new shirt bought for him."

As I come out, I see several people waiting with bundles. Relatives coming to hand in parcels for the dead, the clothes they are to be buried in.

The sun is shining, the sky is copper-sulphate blue. We still have enough of it for a few more baths. A pigeon, arching its back, spreading its tail and cooing, runs around in the roadway, trying to mount two other pigeons at the same time. Through the wide-open windows of the mortuary, I can see a hall with tables and trolleys on which bodies are piled one on top of the other. I see them wheel in Vanya. A young man in a white coat is honing a knife on an electrical whetstone. I want to shout through the window to ask him for something, but don't know what.

The windows in every section of the mortuary are wide open. In the next, a nurse is inputting something on a computer while behind her stands a doctor squeezing her breasts. The nurse giggles, protesting skittishly.

Behind a partition, half a dozen men and women in white coats are merrily drinking away and loud music is playing. Evidently an advance celebration of the New Year. A lively, wrinkled gentleman is jauntily wearing a plastic crown. A corpulent lady is laughing like a drain.

Something comes over me. An unseen force picks me up, sets me in the driving seat of a tank, and shoves the drive levers into my hands. They are the long, crooked teeth of the superannuated scraper of metro posters. I pull the levers and the vehicle clanks forward. The world around me is transformed into a screen image; my thoughts become coded messages transmitted wirelessly. I am a soldier for whom a bombed-out city is just a location on a map, streets littered with corpses mere parallel and intersecting lines.

An obese woman is coming towards me. Round her neck, like a yoke, hangs a big heart made of golden-coloured balloons. It is no easy matter to avoid such a salient object. The balloons rub against me, emitting rubbery squeaks. The woman smiles.

For the weekend, top managers have changed into light sweaters and are out walking with their families. The artificial Christmas trees adorning the squares lift up their tinsel-covered skirts, gold teeth in the mouths of old women have a festive twinkle. I walk on and on...

***

I inform Lena and the sisters. On Lena's recommendation, a lawyer meets with the director of the cemetery. After negotiation, the director agrees to allow Vanya to be buried in our grave, on top of Georgiy Sazonov, artist, although strictly speaking it is illegal.

Sonya and Masha undertake to organize the funeral. I can't sleep. I stagger round the apartment. Outside the windows, fireworks explode and echo. At dawn, I lie down on the couch in the living room.

In the morning, I sit in Vanya's room opposite the window outside which is the hole torn in the advertisement and blue sky. Today we were supposed to hang a piece of bacon fat outside to feed the chicadees. I go to the kitchen, open the fridge, cut a strip off the piece we had prepared, hook it on a piece of wire, and hang it out on the balcony.

I remember that it's time to clean the mushroom. I go to the kitchen, carefully remove the representative of an extraterrestrial civilization from its jar, wash it, and pop it back in.

I look at the ceiling, at the Land of Miracle Yoghurt, its oceans and continents. I see my son, a funny, pudgy little person with a big smile and, for some reason, a tail. Vanya's tail is fluffy, like Churchill's. It is sticking straight up. He is hooting with laughter and skipping around happily.

Oh, we were going to buy a fir tree for New Year's. What should I do now, buy one or not? I mull it over for ages but can't decide.

Vanya, it's your birthday tomorrow, and mine today. We've invited the sisters. What should I do, cancel it? We need to let them know.

A single chicadee flies in to peck at the fat. It turns its little head as it nibbles away. It is pale green. I enjoy looking at it for a while.

What should I do now? I clean both pairs of Vanya's shoes. He only has two pairs. At sixteen, a boy wants to dress attractively but Vanya only has two pairs of shoes you might expect to see on a pensioner.

Vanya, pal, I'd already decided we would live together

for years and years to come. Once we'd rented that apartment out, we'd have had some money. There are so many things I wanted to show you and give you. A cool pair of trainers. We could have gone out, the two of us, dating girls. You're pretty good at that. We might even have gone on a trip to Europe. I'd have shown you the backstreets of Saint-Germain in Paris, we'd have taken a gondola on the green canals of Venice.

My face crumples. I feel like a brimming bowl which may overflow if I make the slightest movement. I go to the bathroom and turn on the taps in order not to be heard. Although, who is there now to hear me? Never mind, I can't cry surrounded by silence. Alone. At least running water is a sound.

The tears come all at once, a lot of tears. I can't see a thing because of them, and to cap it all my nose is running. I empty all the remaining copper sulphate into the bath, undress, and climb in.

"Vanya, you've caught me out again. First you appeared at just the wrong moment and now, just as suddenly, you have gone. You shouldn't do that, with no warning, it isn't fair... Vanya."

I sit in the bathtub, staring fixedly at one spot and rocking, like a Jew at prayer. The blue heap dissolves, giving its colour to the water.

"Please forgive me. Forgive me, Vanya. I don't need anyone other than you. Normal children? What would I need other children for, Vanya? I used to wish I had normal, healthy children but now, after you, what use would they be to me? You loved me the way I am, but normal children would grow up and treat me the way I treated my own parents. They would be ashamed of me. They would be just waiting for the day I gave up my place in life to them."

Mum, Dad, forgive me. How stupidly everything has turned out. Hell, how ridiculously everything has turned out!

I dry my eyes, but immediately new tears come. I wipe those away too. More come.

Drops form on the white ceiling. That means it's hot. Oh yes, I turned on the hot water. There are drops on the wall tiles too. I draw lines with my finger. Other than the sound of running water, there is nothing. A regular, methodical sound. It grows louder.

***

On Vanya's sixteenth birthday, we went to the cemetery to bury him. Before leaving, I pulled the plug out of the bath and the last of the blue water funneled down the drain.

At the mortuary, in the hall for leave-taking, the floor was thick with dust. The room was high-ceilinged and narrow, like a well. The walls were covered with a thick curtaining of some shiny synthetic fabric. Vanya was in a coffin, and it was cold.

"How handsome he is," Masha said.

"He's got a rash on his face. We ate too much sushi," I responded apologetically, like all parents do who are afraid their children are being praised too lavishly.

We drove through the morning city. There were crowds of people around the shops and in the Christmas markets.

"Look, that's my old school," Sonya said, looking out the window. We drove through familiar places. Here I used to play Cossacks and Bandits with my classmates; at this bus stop I used to wait for Lena; this block used to house a big grocery store. When you bought cheese, the sales assistant added a final, very thin slice to get the exact weight. My parents would give that slice to me and I would nibble it on the way home. The huge round cheeses used to have little blue plastic numbers pressed into them, fives and threes. Nobody knew what they were for, but to get a piece of cheese with a number made my day. I would carefully pick them out and store them away, but now I can't remember where. Then that shop was closed and replaced by the first big electronics store in our district. We all went there just to stare in wonder at the tape recorders none of us had seen before. I kept up a running narrative for the sisters. "That's the children's clinic I went to, the video rental shop, the snow slide."

We arrived at the church. The sisters went in to say we were there, while I stayed in the car with Vanya. He doesn't like being left alone.

I examined the coffin. It was all decorated with lacy ruffles, and looked like a dandy with broad shoulders and narrow hips.

In the church, Lena was waiting. She touched my arm but did not remove her dark glasses. I smiled apologetically.

The funeral service. In my left hand I hold a candle, and use the back of my right hand to wipe my nose. I don't have a handkerchief. I've never got the hang of them. Two old women are singing the funeral prayer, and when they cross themselves, their shawls rustle. When I hear that rustling, I know to follow suit and cross myself. While I am doing so, my nose has time to drip. Wipe. Cross. Wipe.

The old women stop singing. "Is that it?" Sonya enquires severely.

"Yes," the old women reply.

"That seemed a bit short."

"What do you mean short? It's according to the Church canon," the old women mumble, offended.

"Then we'll just stand here for a time." Masha snivels.

We admire Vanya. His hair has been styled with gel, like a boy from a good family. I never styled it like that.

We carry the coffin out of the church. I'm holding the end with his head, Sonya and Masha the end with his feet. Lena just walks alongside. When Vanya was born, he was so tiny, and now look how he's grown. He's ten times as tall. A big lad. The old women put an icon on his chest. It is turned to face Vanya, and hence me. I look at Christ and Christ looks back at me.

The guard at the cemetery gate asks loudly, "Soloviov?"

"Yes," Sonya replies.

"Who is Soloviov? Why did Sonya answer 'Yes'?" I wonder in consternation. "Ah, Soloviov is Vanya. He has Lena's surname, from all that time ago at the hospital."

Vanya's lips look as if he has eaten too many blueberries. There are still a few traces of the lipstick. He has long eyelashes. I never noticed that before. His nose is just like mine, and his eyebrows. There's that hair on his chin.

We squeeze past the heroic pilot's railings. The leaves are wet underfoot. Must take care not to slip. Grandpa and Grandma's gravestone has been put back in place. My grandfather looks very serious, his chest covered in medals. He was a Hero of the Soviet Union. Grandma looks loving.

On the damp earth, weeds are growing here and there, pushing through the old leaves, the pine needles and cones. In the grass, a wood screw glitters. There are red eggshells under the bench, dropped there many Easters ago.

A lot is going on in the soil. At first I think I am hallucinating, but looking closer I see a lot of tiny insects, spiders and ants scurrying to and fro, coming to life in the sun. I stop to watch a flat tick, the colour of the soil. It is standing still in the sun, warming first one side, then the other. Occasionally, it changes position and rubs its legs together. I squat down and gently touch it with a twig. It turns over on its back, spreads its legs and pretends to be dead. After a while, it decides the danger has passed, gets up again, and goes back to its sunbathing.

"Bid farewell to the deceased," the gravedigger says quietly. I go to the coffin and look at Vanya. Something has changed in the twig he is still clutching in his hand. At first I am baffled. Oh, look at that. A bud has opened. Amazing! Where before there was a bud, a sticky leaf is now sprouting. Perhaps I just hadn't noticed it before.

I stroke his hand and cover my son with the patchwork rug, folded in quarters, all its hiding places filed with his treasures. Golden spirals, and butterflies, and pearls glisten in the sun. I kiss Vanya on his cheek. It's as if someone has put glasses with thick lenses in front of my eyes which make it difficult to see.

Lena straightens the pillow under Vanya's head. His head turns to one side. She tries to straighten it but it doesn't stay put. She straightens it again and strokes Vanya's arms gently. She lays the painting of Petroleum Venus beside him.

Masha speaks. After being silent for so long, after her tears, her voice is gruff and unsteady. "You remember... he... Vanya likes... on the Internet we... how do you say it in Russian... downloaded... for his birthday we wanted to give him..." Masha takes from her handbag a shiny new mobile phone, presses a button, and it starts to play "Kalinka".

Alack, beneath the pine tree, 'neath the tall,

green pine tree

Take my poor bones and lay me there to rest.

"Good sound quality... polyphonic," Sonya adds.

"Thank you," I say.

"Happy birthday. This is from me and Sonya," Masha says, kissing Vanya twice in the French manner. She puts in a bouquet of purple tulips and the telephone.

Ai, lyuli-lyuli; ai, lyuli-lyuli
Take my poor bones and lay me there to-oo-oo rest!

"Perhaps I should put on some powder to hide the rash. It doesn't look nice…" Masha takes a powder compact from her handbag and masks the rash beside Vanya's lip. We wait.

Sonya sprinkles soil we were given at the church on Vanya in the form of a cross. The soil is wrapped in a grocery invoice. I read, "Buckwheat, 50 kg, 75…" There is a fold in the paper and I can't read the rest of the price. She takes the icon from Vanya's chest and gives it to me.

"It is traditional." I try to blink away the thick lenses covering my eyes. They spill over and are immediately replaced by new ones.

The gravediggers hammer down the coffin lid. A choir sings under the lid as they hammer,

Ka-linka, Kalinka, Kalinka, my love!
Little berry in my orchard, my orchard, my love!
Kalinka, Malinka, Malinka, my love!

I try to find the tick I was observing a couple of minutes ago. I look very closely at the ground where it was basking in the sun. I peer at every blade of grass. No luck. I wipe my eyes. That's enough sentimentality. I need to find that mite. We can't just leave without saying goodbye. I squat down again, scouring every inch. It is nowhere to be seen.

Alongside lies the temporary plaque of George Sazonov and the urns of my parents, dug up for the umpteenth time and waiting to be reinterred. The crumbly red earth thuds down on the coffin. We can no longer hear "Kalinka".

"Till we meet again," I whisper. The gravediggers are expertly firming the sides of the mound the way children pat their sandcastles.

I feel a drop of water on my face. Another.

"Rain," Sonya says absently, holding out her hand. The drops become more frequent. An inoffensive little cloud in the middle of a clear sky suddenly produces a downpour.

I start up my tank and move off. Nobody calls after me. Or perhaps they do and I don't hear. Vanya, I promise not to swear any more, so as not to spoil the karma. I promise to pray and to protect beauty. I know for sure that some day we will become oil. We will splash and gurgle in underground caves and, after millions of years, be found; and pipes will reach down to us like straws and we will be sucked up like fruit juice out of a tumbler. We will flow through pipelines in a thick, oily stream. We will be fractionated, and combusted, and turn into a cloud of exhaust fumes, and fly up into the heavens, there to be inhaled by the Lord God Himself.

In my hand I hold the icon. Thank you, Vanya, for having been here with us. Thank you for having been here with me. Lord, thank you for Vanya having been here with me. Really, it was no ordeal, Lord. Thank you, Lord, for Vanya! Thank you for Vanya! Thank you, and until we meet again. Oh, Lord! Oh, Lord.

***

The city came to life, the spring-like turmoil of the last working day of the year. Denizens scurried back and forth, exactly like the insects in the soil. Hiding from the raindrops, top managers ran into restaurants, girls wearing yoga-pants ran for cover in bus shelters, policemen jumped into their clapped-out Ladas. Old women with gold teeth, the only people to have foreseen the change in the weather, opened umbrellas.

Rain gradually turned to snow. At first, small, but then big, wet snowflakes tumbled out of the sky. They blanketed the swollen buds, the flowering dandelions and daisies, the lush lawns, the flower beds of forget-me-nots, and people wearing ridiculously light clothing.

Walking through an avenue of apple trees, I notice how much the snow on the branches resembles white peonies. The trees have blossomed with white snow peonies. I suddenly have a sense that something inside me has disappeared. I have jettisoned some great ballast. Fears. I no longer fear anything. I was once afraid I would never have a healthy child. I was afraid of schoolteachers, prison, the police. I was afraid of poverty, unemployment, and impotence. I was afraid of cancer, AIDS, torture, like having my eyes put out and needles pushed under my fingernails. I was afraid of the dark, of cockroaches, of the monsters in "Alien". I was afraid of being Vanya's nursemaid for the rest of my life.

I am no longer afraid of anything.

I am no longer afraid of losing my friends, not having a successful career, or not living a vivid enough life. So this is freedom! Not freedom from a disabled son, which I tried for so long to clutch at, but freedom from everything. I no longer love and I also have no hatred. I am not envious, do not fuss, do not expect anything, and do not believe. I have no faith, only a happy serenity. The abyss is in front of me. I look into it, unflinching, and because of that I am happy. Vanya took me right to the brink of the abyss and now has set me free. Hi, abyss, it's me, right here in front of you.

Drivers warm up their snow-covered cars. They look as if the fuming exhaust pipes are sticking out of snowdrifts, and the bright headlights are the lit-up windows in Eskimos' igloos. Schoolchildren roll huge snowballs in order to make a snowman with an ear-to-ear smile. The snow-clearing vehicles, which for so long stood idle, now crawl out onto the streets, their engines roaring. The communal utilities react quickly and catch the snow almost before it falls.

Workers in orange overalls, with broad faces and shovels, help dig out vehicles.

One workman is driving a small digger, while another shovels snow from hard to reach places into its scoop. Two girl students wearing short skirts cross the pavement. The guy with the shovel is clearing snow from under the wheel of a parked car and doesn't see their shapely legs. The guy operating the digger honks his horn. The guy with the shovel looks up. The guy in the digger nods in the direction of the students. They grin after the receding legs.

As I walk past, I catch the eye of the guy in the digger. He smiles, as if to say, did you see that? He wants to share a life-enhancing moment with me.

I smile back. Yes, I sure did!